Veronica Ganz

Veronica Ganz

by Marilyn Sachs

illustrated by Louis Glanzman

A Yearling Book

Published by
Dell Publishing Co., Inc.
1 Dag Hammarskjold Plaza
New York, New York 10017

Yearling ® TM 913705, Dell Publishing Co., Inc.

ISBN: 0-440-49205-X

Reprinted by arrangement with
Doubleday & Company, Inc.

Printed in the United States of America
Second Dell Printing—September 1978

To Anne Jackson, whose generous and wise teaching turned so many of us into children's librarians, and whose friendship remains a wonder and a joy.

Veronica Ganz

1

"Veronica Ganz
Doesn't wear pants.
Veronica Ganz
Doesn't wear pants."

They had just passed the fish store on Boston Road when they heard it. Veronica gripped Mary Rose's arm and whispered, "Keep walking!"

"Aw, Veronica," Mary Rose began whining, "just forget it today. Stanley's waiting for us, and Mama left a quarter on the table, and the place closes at four-thirty. Please Veronica, not today, Veronica."

But Veronica just gave her one look, that familiar look, and Mary Rose started whimpering, "Why are you looking at me like that? It's not my fault."

"Just shut up, and keep walking," Veronica hissed. She slowed her pace, and waited. Sure enough, it came again, louder and clearer this time.

> "Veronica Ganz
> Doesn't wear pants.
> Oh—Veronica Ganz
> Doesn't wear pants."

"Peter Wedemeyer," Veronica said decisively. "I'll kill him."

"How do you know it's him?" said Mary Rose.

"Because he lisps," said Veronica. "Can't you hear? He says, 'Veronica Ganth, doethn't wear panth.' It's him all right."

"But where is he?"

Veronica cast a quick look over her shoulder. "Behind the ice truck in front of the fish store. You can see his feet. Just wait till I get my hands on him!"

She looked around her again with an experienced eye, examining the terrain. "O.K., Mary Rose, listen! Here's the candy store. Let's make believe we're going inside." She turned Mary Rose toward the store and slowly, very slowly, so that Peter was sure to see them, she began walking toward the entrance. "We'll wait till he says it again. He'll stick his head out to say it, and then duck back again. As soon as he does, I'll sneak up the block, cross the street, and double back on him from there. Meanwhile, you stand here and keep looking in the store like you're waiting for me. Kind of stamp your foot once in a while like you're sick of waiting, and maybe even yell 'Veronica,' and I'll—"

"*Veronica Ganz
Doesn't wear pants.*"

Veronica flew up the block, crossed the street, and, stooping low on the sidewalk behind the parked cars there, began tracking her quarry. She could see him now, very clearly, hiding behind the ice truck, and peeking out every once in a while. There was Mary Rose in front of the candy store, playing decoy. Good old Mary Rose! Even though she was a fink, in moments like this, she sure was a help. Carefully Veronica moved silently along, narrowing the distance between Peter and herself.

"Hey, Veronica, what are you doing?"

There was Rita Ferguson standing there, grinning. Big mouth! "Get lost!" Veronica snapped, and made a little move toward her. Rita went scuttling off down the street. Now for Peter. He's been asking for it, Veronica reflected, as she continued padding along behind the cars. Peter was a new kid in her class, new in the neighborhood, too. He and she hadn't been properly introduced, she thought with a grim smile, and lately some troublesome things had been happening. Somebody kept throwing her coat off the hook in the clothes closet, and somebody had put a tack on her seat this morning. She'd had her suspicions all right. Nobody else in the class would dare to tangle with her. They'd all been through it already one way or another. But every new kid, sooner or later, had to be educated. The girls were easy. They'd giggle or whisper about her, and generally one loud slap in the face kept them in line. She didn't really enjoy fighting girls. They just stood there and cried. Boys were more interesting. Frank Scacalossi, for instance—he'd been interesting, and harder to beat than anyone else. Probably what she ought to do, as soon as a new kid arrived, was right away give him a poke in the nose so there wouldn't be any question in his mind about who she was. Not that she really minded a good fight with all the trimmings, but some days it just was not as convenient as others. Now today, it was not convenient at all, but maybe if she got it over with quickly, she and Mary Rose could still get over to the day-old bakery.

Carefully she raised her head from behind the blue Chevy and gazed thoughtfully at Peter's back. She was in a direct line with him now, and it was just a question of whether she should rush out at him from where she was standing, or continue up the block and make a charge on his right flank. More cautious that way, of course, but today she just did not have all the time in the world. She'd take a chance. Besides, if she caught him head on she could just drive him against the truck, which would be a convenient place to hold him and bang his head.

She looked up and down the street. No cars. Here goes! She flew out from behind the car, dashed across the street, and grabbed Peter just as he was beginning to poke his head around the side of the truck and holler. In fact, his mouth was halfway open, and his beginning cry of "Ver . . ." was shouted, but never finished, into Veronica's grinning face.

"Did you call?" Veronica inquired politely, as she lined Peter up against the back of the truck and banged his head against it.

Peter closed his mouth. His face turned pasty. This would not take too long, Veronica knew.

"Well, here I am," said Veronica, banging his head again. A few more bangs, one or two pokes, and it would be over. But Peter kicked her hard in the shins and flew off into the sanctuary of the fish store.

That lousy little shrimp! Veronica thought, standing uncertainly in front of the fish store and gazing inside. He kicked me. Peter was the smallest kid in the class, but Veronica knew that size was no measure of a challenger's mettle. It was frequently the little kids who gave her the most trouble. Howard Tannenbaum, now, another shrimp, and only in the seventh grade, had cut her lip so badly last month that she hadn't been able to chew for a couple of days. Of course, a cut lip was nothing compared to what she had done to Howard. But that was all water under the bridge, and right now Peter was hiding in the fish store, and how was she going to get him out?

She snapped her fingers at Mary Rose, who was

still standing near the candy store. Mary Rose came running.

"Where'd he go?" she asked. "What happened?"

"In there," Veronica said. "He kicked me. Oh, will he be sorry! Now, go inside, and tell him to come out. Tell him I'm waiting, and I don't have all day."

Mary Rose entered the fish store. In a minute, she was back. "He won't come."

"Tell him," said Veronica, "if he doesn't come out, I'll come in and get him."

"He said come and get him," Mary Rose said, reporting back.

Veronica weighed the various possibilities. She could just stand around and wait for him to come out. Sooner or later, he'd have to come out. Or, she could go in and get him. Trouble with that was there were grownups inside who were certain to break it up, and equally certain to yell at her, and call her a bully, and tell her to pick on someone her own size even though he had started it. Or she could wait until tomorrow and catch him on the way to school.

"Come on, Veronica," pleaded Mary Rose, "let's go home. You can get him tomorrow."

She looked up at Mary Rose's anxious face in distaste. Her mind was made up. She'd get him today. Maybe somebody would break it up, but not before she'd given him a few wallops he wouldn't forget in a hurry.

She strode into the store. The fish man was busy

waiting on a woman, and another customer was in-
specting the gills of a big fish lying on the ice.
Peter was crouched down at the end of the counter.
Jerk! Veronica thought. Does he think I don't see
him there?

"Come on, Peter," Veronica crooned, walking
quickly toward him. "Come on home, Peter. Mama's
got a nice bottle of milk waiting for you. Come on,
baby."

Peter stood up and waved. Funny kid! "Come and
get me," he said, grinning.

Veronica smiled a wide, loving smile, and rushed
forward with both arms outstretched. She saw him
stoop down, and just as her fingers were beginning
to close on his shoulders—*whish*, it was suddenly
dark. She stood there choking and gasping, and
struggling to breathe under the waste bucket Peter
had thrown over her head. On her nose, her mouth,
on her shoulders, up and down her arms and legs,
a cascade of scales, fish heads, tails, and other odor-
iferous fish leavings enveloped her. She yanked the
bucket off her head, and the smell and the feel of
being encased in decaying fish was too much for her.

"Aaaah, aaaah, aaaah!" she shrieked.

"Whatsamatter? Whatsamatter?" yelled the fish
man, darting toward her. "You crazy kids—get out of
here!"

"My goodness, what will they think of next," said
one customer.

"It's a disgrace," murmured the woman who had

been examining the fish's gills, and was now looking into its eyes.

Veronica fled, leaving a trail of fish behind her. Outside, Peter was already nearly at the corner, and she flew after him, shouting, "Peter Wedemeyer, Peter Wedemeyer, I'll get you, Peter Wedemeyer!"

Peter kept running. Behind her she could hear Mary Rose calling, but she didn't turn around. Nobody had ever done anything like this to her in her whole life. When Sanford Feldman had pushed her into Indian Lake it was nothing compared to this. Besides, she had been holding Sanford.

Swiftly, Peter fled down Boston Road, and hot on his trail flew Veronica. Faster and faster her long legs beat on the pavement, and smaller and smaller grew the distance between them.

She lost sight of him just for a moment when he turned on Clinton Avenue, but she saw him again as she sped around the corner. There he was, less than half a block away. Another burst of speed, and she'd have him. But suddenly Peter darted up the stairs of an apartment house and disappeared inside. Good, good! Let him hide inside. She'd find him, and drag him out, and let him scream his head off, once she had him, he was hers. Up the stairs Veronica ran, into the building, and immediately raced for the bottom of the stairwell. Peter was not there. She raced up the stairs, pausing at each landing to look, but Peter had disappeared. The door to the roof was locked, so he hadn't gone there. Where was he then? Where was he hiding?

"Peter Wedemeyer," she boomed into the heart of the silent building, "wherever you are, I'll find you." Quickly she descended and stood at the bottom of the staircase, breathing very hard, with her heart thumping loudly in her chest. How could he have disappeared? Where did he go? Oh no! Not that! It couldn't be!

She charged over to the mailboxes in the vestibule and inspected the names under them. WEDEMEYER–APT. 3A. This was the house he lived in.

Veronica sat down on the floor, put her right hand over her heart, and raised her left hand in the air. "I swear to God I'll get Peter Wedemeyer," she chanted. "And if I don't, may I fall down dead, and–" Mary Rose opened the outside door and gaped at her. "And may Mary Rose fall down dead." (Mary Rose started crying.) "And may Stanley fall down dead, and may Ralph fall down dead, and may . . ." No, there was no need to add Mama to the list. It would do. "May we all fall down dead if I don't get Peter Wedemeyer."

"What happened?" Mary Rose sobbed. "I wanna go home." Suddenly she stopped sobbing, and a weak little smile began growing on her face until it blossomed into a wide, wondering laugh. "You got a fish head in your hair, and . . ." Mary Rose sniffed the air. "What's that funny smell?"

With a cry of fury, Veronica leaped up and ran

back into the hall—3A, that's where he lived, 3A.
She passed 1A, 2A, and stood, snorting, in front of
the innocent-looking green door marked 3A. She
knocked at the door. Nobody answered. She rang
the bell. Nobody answered. She kicked the door,
and leaned on the bell.

"Go 'way," said a voice from behind the door.

"Open up this door," shouted Veronica, struggling
to turn the knob, which of course refused to turn.

"Go 'way," said Peter.

"Let me in," Veronica cried, pounding on the door,
"or—"

And there was Peter, laughing. She and Mary Rose
could hear him clearly, laughing. "Or," he cried,
"you'll huff and you'll puff, and you'll blow the
house down. Ha, ha, ha, ha. Hee, hee, hee . . ."
They heard a thump, and the laughter coming from
lower down behind the door where Peter had fallen,
roaring with laughter.

Veronica began to fling herself against the door,
but the door to Apartment 2A opened and a woman
came out into the hall.

"What are you doing to that door, little girl?"
she said. "What's going on here?"

Veronica continued flinging herself against the
door.

"Now stop that!" the woman said sharply. "Stop
that right now!"

"Mrs. Rizzio," came Peter's voice from behind the
door, sounding very high and frightened. "Please,

Mrs. Rizzio, make her go away. My mother's not home, and she wants to hurt me. She's the biggest bully in the world, and she followed me home from school, and . . . oh, please, Mrs. Rizzio," Peter was sobbing now. "I'm all alone, and I'm so scared."

Mrs. Rizzio grabbed Veronica's shoulders and began shaking her. "Shame on you, shame!" she cried. "You big bully, picking on a nice little boy like Peter Wedemeyer."

"Nice little boy!" yelled Veronica. "He started it. He—"

"Now go home, go home!" shrilled Mrs. Rizzio, dragging her toward the door. "Go home, and don't let me see you here again." She stopped for a moment and sniffed the air. "What's that terrible smell? Phew!"

"He threw fish on me," Veronica began. "He—"

"Fish, tish," scolded Mrs. Rizzio. "A big girl like you. Take a bath, that's what you should do instead of picking on little kids and telling lies. Clean yourself up, and don't go around smelling like that. If you go around smelling like that, nobody'll ever marry you. You'll see."

She opened the door, pushed Veronica out on the stoop, waited for Mary Rose to follow, and then slammed the door.

"C'mon, Veronica," Mary Rose whined, "let's go home."

"I'm not going home!" Veronica said, sitting down on the stoop. "I'll wait here all night for him. I'll stay here till he comes out. I'll catch him. I'll fix him. I'll—"

Mrs. Rizzio opened the door and waved her hand a few times. "Go!" she ordered. "Go!"

Veronica stayed where she was.

"I'm calling the police," Mrs. Rizzio said.

Veronica got up, and walked quickly down the stairs, and up the block.

"Tomorrow's another day," Mary Rose said soothingly, walking beside her. She pulled the fish head from Veronica's hair, tittered, and began brushing the scales and fish pieces off her jacket.

"What's so funny?" Veronica snarled, raising her hand. But Mary Rose tittered again, and quickly fled up the block, and around the corner.

"Fink!" Veronica muttered. But she was too tired to give chase. Now all she wanted to do was get home and, as Mrs. Rizzio had suggested, take a bath and separate herself from that horrible smell of fish that enveloped her.

> "*Veronica Ganz*
> *Doesn't wear pants.*
> *Veronica Ganz*
> *Doesn't wear pants.*"

Veronica knew that she should just ignore him now. Just keep on walking, and later at home, when she was cool, calm, collected, and clean, she could lay out a reasonable plan of revenge. But revenge was not the only issue at stake here. There was also this matter of whether she did or did not wear pants. And she always did wear pants. So she turned and looked back at Peter Wedemeyer, who was leaning half out of his window, and she shouted back at him, "Peter Wedemeyer, you liar! I do so wear pants." And quickly she flipped her skirt up to her waist, revealing the pair of pink panties that lay underneath. Then she dropped her skirt, shook her fist at him, and said, "I'll get you tomorrow."

And with that question cleared up, she turned and began walking again toward the corner. A moment of silence, and then,

> "*Veronica Ganz*
> *Has ants in her pants.*"

But Veronica just hurried along. Tomorrow was another day.

2

Stanley was sitting on the stoop waiting, and as soon as he saw her he jumped up and began shouting something she couldn't hear. As she drew closer, she could see that he looked even messier than usual—his hair stood up in points on his head, his shoes were untied, the buttons were off his jacket, and as usual his nose was running.

"Go 'way," she snapped, as soon as they were close enough for him to hear her.

But Stanley's face was shining with pleasure. "Can we go now, Veronica?" he continued shouting even though there was no longer any need to shout. "Right now? I'm ready, Veronica."

Veronica walked right past him through the door
to the apartment house and began climbing the three
flights of stairs. Stanley followed along right behind
her.

"What took you so long, Veronica? I've been waiting and waiting. Mary Rose is home. Can we go
now? What smells so funny? Veronica, are you ready?
Can we go? I want a chocolate marshmallow cake
with a nut on it, and Papa likes to have a lemon
coconut cake. Mama said so. Are you ready, Veronica?
Can we go now?"

Veronica opened the door that said 4D on it, and
R. PETRONSKI under it, entered the apartment, and
slammed the door behind her. She nearly tripped
over a bundle that stood in the hall, and, grumbling,
she kicked at it and continued on into the kitchen.

Mama had promised to leave a quarter for them
on the kitchen table, and it was there, all right. The
note under it said:

> V.—
>   Make sure to get a lemon coconut cake for R.
> and anything else you like.
>   M.

The clock over the refrigerator said four-ten. Well
that was just great, wasn't it. For a quarter they
could have gotten a bag full of cake at the day-old
bakery—enough to have a real feast tonight, with
plenty left over for several days. But the place was

down on Third Avenue, and took at least half an hour to walk to, and closed at four-thirty sharp. So they'd have to wait until tomorrow, and eat graham crackers tonight. Oh—what she'd do to Peter when she caught him.

The door opened, and Stanley came in, still talking. "Didn't know where you were.. But now we can go. Right, Veronica?"

What a pest! "Look," snapped Veronica, "we're not going today. It's too late. So go away and stop bothering me."

Stanley's happy smile dissolved. "I wanted a chocolate marshmallow cake with a nut on it," he crooned, and immediately began hiccuping.

Veronica brushed by him impatiently, strode through the living room, and into the bedroom she and Mary Rose shared. Mary Rose was lying on the unmade bed, the blankets on the floor, examining something she had laid out on the bed.

"Look, Veronica," she said happily. "They came today in the mail." On the sheet were lying about thirty cardboard fingernails in different shades of red, pink, and orange. Mary Rose was always mailing away for things—samples of lipstick, perfumes, face powders, interior decorating charts, soaps. She picked a bright pink nail up, inspected it, and sighed. "Isn't this the most gorgeous color you ever saw in your life?"

"Get them off my side of the bed!" Veronica thundered.

Mary Rose made a face, gave a meaningful sniff at the air, opened the window emphatically, but she moved all the fingernails to her side of the bed.

Stanley stood in the doorway, hiccuping.

"Is he starting that again?" Mary Rose said, disdainfully.

Veronica just pulled out her drawer in the chest and began hunting for some clean underwear. There were some socks in the drawer, but no underwear.

"Where's my underwear?" Veronica shouted, pushing all the socks around desperately.

Stanley said, between hiccups, "There's a bundle of wet wash in the hall. Mama left it—*hic*—before she—*hic*—went to the store. She said you—*hic*—should hang it out. What's that funny smell—*hic*—Veronica?"

"Go away," Mary Rose said. "Don't hiccup in my room."

Veronica slammed the drawer, hurried back through the living room into the hall, and opened the bundle. Everything was wet and clammy, but she dug down through the layers of clothes until she found an undershirt and a pair of panties. She laid them on top of the radiator, and shouted, "Mary Rose, hang up the laundry!"

No answer.

"*MARY ROSE*," bellowed Veronica, "I said hang up the wash."

"Oh, O.K.," came the distant, dreamy voice from the bedroom.

Veronica began pulling her clothes off almost before she got into the bathroom. She closed the door, ran the water full blast in the tub, and climbed in as soon as she had stripped. But the pile of clothes on the bathroom floor smelled up the whole room, so she rose, dripping from the tub, opened the door, and flung the clothes outside. Stanley was standing there, and she banged the door in his face and hooked the latch.

The water felt warm and clean and comforting. She put her head under the water and scrubbed until all the scales were floating lazily in the tub. She had to let fresh water in twice more before she could lean back in the clean, warm, still slightly smelly water, and think pleasant thoughts about what Peter would look like with two black eyes and a bloody nose.

But her reveries were interrupted. Somebody was hiccuping outside her door.

"Stanley," she yelled, "stop hiccuping outside my door. Go hiccup somewhere else."

"Where?" Stanley asked.

"How should I know. But get away from that door."

Stanley sniffed. "Where should I go?" he said sadly. "Mary Rose won't let me hiccup in her room, you won't let me hiccup here. Where should I go?"

"Go to the kitchen!" Veronica screamed.

"Oh, O.K." The hiccuping on the other side of the door stopped, and again Veronica lay back in the

tub and tried to compose her thoughts. Where was
she? That Stanley—he never left her alone for a
minute. And those hiccups of his! Once he started,
he could go on like that for hours, sometimes even
days. Once he got upset over something, you could
count on it. He wouldn't yell or scream or hit—just
hiccup. And his sad, pale eyes kept blinking, and
blinking.

He's just like his father, she thought scornfully.
And then feeling ashamed, she turned over on her
stomach and ducked her head under the water. Not
that Ralph was really such a bad egg, she didn't
mean to think that. Some kids who had stepfathers
complained about how mean they were and how they
liked their own kids better. Ralph wasn't like that
at all. She could still remember when he started
coming around, courting Mama. He wore a big button on his coat, and he told her it said "Vote for
Franklin D. Roosevelt for a New Deal." He said if
Franklin D. Roosevelt was elected President nobody
would be poor any more. And one day, because she
liked it so much, Ralph took off the button and
pinned it on Veronica's dress and said she could
keep it. She was five then, as old as Stanley now,
and Mary Rose was three. He always brought them
candy, and let them sit on his lap, and climb all
over him, and never scolded them, just grinned at
them with those big, pale, blinking eyes, like Stanley.
That was over eight years ago, and now she was
thirteen, and Mary Rose was eleven, and he still

brought them candy, and even though they didn't sit on his lap any more, he still never scolded them or hit them. He had a soft, slow voice, and when he was upset, like Stanley, he didn't lose his temper or scream. He just spoke very, very slowly, and his pale eyes grew sad.

"Spineless," Mama said sometimes, when she was angry at him, and people took advantage of him. Not a day passed that Mama didn't come home from the store, sore at Ralph. It might be that a customer said there were holes in a garment after it came back from the cleaners, when all the time, Mama said, that customer knew very well those holes were there before. Or somebody was in a big hurry to have something pressed and Ralph stayed late. Or Jerry, the high school boy who worked for them after school, didn't show up but Ralph paid him anyway—always something.

Before Ralph married Mama, he used to be a presser in a big cleaning store, but Mama had persuaded him to open his own store. It was a little store on Prospect Avenue, and most every day Mama worked there too. Before Stanley started kindergarten, Mama would take him along to the store, and he played there the whole day. But now that he was in school in the mornings, he just went over there for lunch. There was a hot plate in back of the store, and Mama made lunch for him. Then he generally liked to come home and wait for her and Mary Rose.

"It won't hurt you to keep an eye on him," Mama said, and if they kept arguing with her, boy, would she scream. Mama screamed a lot, and hit, too, when she was real mad. Ralph would generally get nervous when she did, and say something like, "Don't get mad, Peggy. They're just kids." He'd always try to work out some kind of a compromise so that everybody would be happy, but it was Mama who generally had the last word.

Just this morning at breakfast, Mama had exploded. Stanley was eating toast and cream cheese, and his whole face was covered with it. Mary Rose looked at him and said, "Uuk," and made a sort of throwing-up noise. And Mama got right up and whacked her one across the face. And Mary Rose started crying. And Mama began yelling about how she was always picking on him and what a selfish brat she was. And Ralph said, "What are you hitting her for? She didn't mean anything." Then, boy, did Mama let him have it.

"You're some big hero, aren't you?" she yelled. "Always taking somebody else's part. Why don't you take my part for a change? Where were you yesterday when that Mr. Wittenberg called me a liar in the store—right in front of you too."

"But you said he was a crook first, and you said he . . ."

But Mama began yelling so loud then that both Ralph and Mary Rose ran out of the room.

Veronica climbed out of the tub, wrapped a towel around her, and came out into the living room to check her underwear on the radiator. It was still damp on one side so she turned it over, and sniffed the pleasant smell of clean clothes drying. There was a pile of newspapers and magazines on the coffee table, and on top of them were some letters. Veronica picked them up and looked them over. Not that she was expecting anything. She never sent away for any of that junk Mary Rose collected. There was a gas bill, and another letter to Ralph from the American Legion, and a letter to Mama.

"Mary Rose," Veronica screamed, "you didn't tell me there was a letter from Papa."

"There is?" Mary Rose cried, hurrying from the bedroom. "I didn't notice the other things when I brought the mail up. I was so busy looking at the fingernails."

She took the letter out of Veronica's hand and inspected it. Sure enough, it was addressed to Mrs. Ralph Petronski, and the return address said F. Ganz, 35 Laurel Dr., Las Vegas, Nevada.

"Gee!" Mary Rose said. "It's not Christmas yet. He never writes to Mama in between."

Veronica took the letter back, and she and Mary Rose sat down on the couch and looked at it.

"What do you think?" Mary Rose said softly.

Stanley came into the room, still hiccuping. "Can we go tomorrow?" he pleaded. Nobody answered him, so he moved the pile of jackets away and sat down next to Veronica. "What's that?" he asked, pointing to the letter.

"It's a letter," Mary Rose said loftily, "from *our* Papa."

"From Papa?"

"From *our* Papa," Mary Rose continued patiently. Stanley always forgot. "Your Papa is Ralph but our Papa is Frank Ganz, who lives on 35 Laurel Drive in Las Vegas, Nevada."

"Is he dead?" Stanley said thoughtfully.

"No, he's not dead," Mary Rose snapped. "You always say that. Why can't you understand? Mama was married to our Papa before she married Ralph. They got a divorce. I keep telling you."

She took the letter back from Veronica and held it up. "There's a lot of writing inside." She licked her lips. "I wonder what it says." She looked at Veronica, just waiting.

"No," Veronica said weakly. "Mama'll be home soon. Better wait and let her read it first." They looked at each other, but then the door opened, and Stanley jumped up, and ran out of the room, yelling and hiccuping, "Mama, Mama, we didn't go to the day-old bakery. Mama . . ."

There was a rustling and a thump in the kitchen, where Mama must have put down her packages. They heard the water running, and Mama saying to Stanley, "Drink it up." Then she walked into the living room.

"Why is he hiccuping?" she asked. "What did you do to him?"

"Nothing, Mama," Mary Rose cried. "There's a letter from Papa." She jumped up from the couch and ran over to Mama with the letter in her hand.

"From Frank?" Mama said, surprised. "What in the world?"

She opened it and began reading. Veronica got up and walked over to her, and waited. Mama turned the first page, her eyes darting quickly back and forth as she read. There was another page, but Mama didn't read that. She just stopped reading, and looked worried. "Your father," she said, "he's coming next week—with his wife."

3

After supper, Mama and Ralph went into the kitchen and shut the door. But first, Mama said, "You can put Stanley to bed tonight."

Mary Rose immediately got up and walked off.

"Who, me?" Veronica said.

"Yes, you."

"Why me?" Veronica grumbled. "Why do I have to always be the one?"

"You aren't always the one," Mama began talking, her voice rising higher and higher as she spoke. "You hardly ever do it, but tonight you have to do it because I SAID SO." She slammed the kitchen door.

Stanley was sitting on the floor in his parents'

bedroom when Veronica stamped into the room. He had two decks of cards spread out around him and was trying to match all the same ones together. He was holding the jack of hearts in his hand and looking around for its mate.

"Pick those cards up off the floor," Veronica said, "and get into your pajamas."

Stanley looked happy. "You putting me to bed, Veronica?"

Veronica began pulling Stanley's trundle bed out from under the big bed. "Get a move on," she said. "I've got things to do."

"Sure, Veronica, sure." Stanley quickly began gathering all his cards together. "I'm glad you're putting me to bed. I like when you put me to bed."

Veronica took the blanket and pillow out of the closet. "Come on, hurry," she said, "and go to the bathroom first."

When Stanley came back, he pulled all his clothes off and dropped them on the floor.

"What's that?" Veronica said, pointing to a red circle on his shoulder.

"Where? Oh, that. That's where Jimmy Reilly bit me."

"Bit you? Why'd he bite you?"

"He always bites me," Stanley said in a melancholy voice.

"And what do you do when he bites you?"

"I tell him, 'Stop it!' But he won't."

Veronica exploded. "You're such a spineless little coward," she screamed at him. "That's why they're always hitting you, and pushing you, and biting you. You're the biggest kid in your class, and everybody picks on you, and you never lift a finger. Why didn't you hit him back?"

Stanley's big eyes blinked and blinked. "Maybe tomorrow," he said softly. "Maybe tomorrow I'll hit him back."

"Sure, sure," Veronica sneered, "tomorrow you'll hit him back! Baloney! If it wasn't for me, they'd tear you to pieces, and you'd let them." She put her face up close to his. "I've always got to be pulling some kid or other off you, and I don't like smacking little kids."

"So why do you do it?" Stanley said, moving his head back a little.

"Because you don't do it for yourself. But after this, I'm finished. Whatever happens to you, I'm not going to lift a finger to help you. Do you hear me?"

"O.K., Veronica," Stanley said meekly. He touched the bite on his shoulder. "It doesn't really hurt so much, any more." He drew his pajamas on, crept into his bed, and pulled the covers up to his chin.

"Good night!" Veronica said, putting out the light.

"Veronica!"

"What?"

"Tell me a story."

"Not tonight," said Veronica. "I'm busy." She began walking out the door, and a gentle hiccup followed her. Oh, that rotten kid! He'll start hiccuping again, and Mama'll chew my head off.

"All right, all right," Veronica snapped, coming back into the room. "Just stop hiccuping."

"I'll try." Stanley hicced again.

Veronica sat down on the big bed.

"Tell me the one about Bluebeard," Stanley pleaded.

"Oh, all right. Just don't hiccup."

"I won't," Stanley said in a strangled voice between his teeth.

"Once upon a time," said Veronica quickly, "there was a man named Bluebeard because he had a beard that was so black it looked blue. And he came to a country where nobody knew him. And he married a beautiful girl named . . . named . . ."

"Veronica," Stanley offered.

"No, Loretta. So he took her home to his house. It was a great big house, kind of dark, and smelly, and gloomy."

"Like school?"

"No, bigger, and gloomier, and smellier. And he gave her a bunch of keys and said she could look in every room in the house except the one up in the attic. But one day, when he wasn't home—"

"Veronica," Stanley said, "come and sit on my bed."

Veronica bent down and sat on the edge of Stanley's bed, and Stanley turned over on his side with his face against her leg, and one arm in her lap.

"Well, so he wasn't home, and she opened the door to the room in the attic, and she saw—"

"Bodies," Stanley said contentedly, "lots of bodies."

"All over the place," Veronica continued. "And some had their heads off, and some had their arms and legs off, and pieces of ladies were hanging up all over the walls."

Veronica began describing all the horrors the room contained, and Stanley nestled closer and closer to her. Her voice grew low as she told how Loretta sent a message to her brothers, big, strong men—

"Like Papa?" Stanley suggested.

Veronica let that pass without comment, and went on to tell how Bluebeard discovered that Loretta had been in the room. How he told her to prepare to die. How she stalled for time. How her brothers arrived just as Bluebeard was chasing her around the kitchen table, and proceeded to hack him into many pieces.

"How many?" Stanley asked.

"Oh, lots and lots."

"Maybe a thousand," Stanley murmured happily, without a single hiccup.

"Maybe," Veronica said agreeably. Stanley's hand was in hers by this time, and his head was in her lap. She couldn't see his face in the darkness, and maybe that was why she forgot to be sore at him.

Gently, she put his hand down, stood up, and walked quietly to the door.

"Veronica!"

"Now what?"

"I'm scared."

"What of?"

"That window shade," Stanley murmured. "It keeps flapping."

Veronica pulled the window shade down below the level of the window and started out once more.

"Veronica!"

"What?"

"That was a nice story, Veronica," Stanley said sleepily.

"Good night," said Veronica, closing the door. She made a mental note to catch Jimmy Reilly tomorrow and give him a few slaps for biting Stanley.

Mary Rose wasn't in their bedroom, and she wasn't in the bathroom either. Veronica looked in the living room. She wasn't there either, but was crouched down behind the kitchen door, listening. She grinned when she saw Veronica, put her finger to her lips, and softly, on stockinged feet, tiptoed back into the living room.

"Let's go in the bedroom," she whispered.

Aside from being the biggest fink in the world, Mary Rose was also the biggest sneak. Always listening in on private conversations. And if it was not for all the useful and amazing bits of information she acquired that way, Veronica would have refused

to listen to her. As a rule Veronica held a very low opinion of sneaks, finks, and liars. *She* never lied, and *she* never sneaked, and, especially, *she* never, never finked. People might say she was a bully, but she knew very well that she wasn't that either. Nobody could say she ever started a fight—at least not without a good reason—but she could always be counted on to finish a fight. And what was wrong with that? If she didn't take care of herself, and make sure that nobody picked on her, who would take care of her? Or of Stanley? Or of Mary Rose, too, for that matter? All she wanted was for people to leave her and her family alone, and not to make fun of them. Why should that make her a bully?

She followed Mary Rose into their bedroom and waited while she closed the door. Mary Rose's cheeks were flushed, and her eyes were shining. She looked almost pretty. She always seemed to look her best when she had been listening in on something she wasn't supposed to hear.

"Boy, is Mama upset," she said, gloating. "Wait'll you hear what she said."

"One of these days," Veronica said, almost lecturing, "Mama'll catch you sneaking around like that, and she'll knock your head off."

"Oh, she never has." Mary Rose shook her head impatiently. "But you know what—I think he's got lots of money."

"Who has?"

"Papa. Our Papa. And Mama said she wouldn't take a single penny from him. And she said he sold his restaurant in Las Vegas, and he's going to live on a ranch, and she says he wants to steal us away from her."

"What?"

"Swear to God she said that—or something like that," Mary Rose said solemnly. "Because they don't have any children, and they've been married a long time so it must be that they can't have any. And I'll bet that's why they're coming here—to take us back with them." Mary Rose began squealing, "Isn't that marvelous? Our Papa's rich, and he has a ranch with horses, I bet—oh—I can't wait to go."

Veronica sat down on the bed. "So where's he been all these years?" she said doubtfully. "How come he didn't come to see us before if he wants us so much? Phooey, I don't believe it."

"I don't know," Mary Rose shrugged. "Maybe he just couldn't come. Maybe his wife was sick. Maybe he had to work in the restaurant all the time. Who cares? But he's coming now, and I can't wait to go back with him. I hate this dump, don't you?"

Veronica didn't say anything, but she was beginning to feel a funny, jumping flutter in her stomach.

"Why should we stay here?" Mary Rose began whining. "Nobody cares for us here. Mama doesn't really love us. You know—she just loves Stanley—not us."

"Oh, cut it out," Veronica snapped. Mary Rose was always going on and on about who loved who more than who, and how this one didn't love her as much as that one—it was sickening.

"I wonder what she looks like—his wife, I mean. Helen's such a pretty name, isn't it? I bet she's beautiful. I kind of think of her as a blonde with blue eyes—like Lorraine Day. And Papa's so handsome." Mary Rose opened the bottom drawer of the chest and pulled out the picture. She sat down next to Veronica, and they studied it, as they had many times before. It was their parents' wedding picture, and their father looked very tall, and blond, and handsome in his tuxedo. "He must be as tall as Ralph," Mary Rose whispered, "but he's all muscle. Just look at his shoulders."

In the picture Mama looked pretty much as she looked today, but younger, and her hair was all fancy on top of her head. Her veil was thrown back and she wore a long satin gown and held flowers in her hand. She looked very happy. And when Veronica saw that young, smiling face of Mama's, she felt like hitting someone—the same way she felt when someone had hurt Stanley. Because there was something else she remembered. Something that had happened a long time ago, but Mama's face was very clear in her mind, as clear as it was in the picture. They were riding on the subway. Mama was holding a baby in her lap—it must have been Mary Rose, and she was sitting next to Mama.

And Mama began to cry. Somebody who was sitting on the other side of Mama said, "Stop it! Everybody's looking at you." But Mama kept crying and crying. She could hear the voice in her mind. It was a man's voice, but that was all she remembered.

"You know," Mary Rose whispered, "I bet it was like that movie, *Stella Dallas.* You know, Papa was rich, and he came from a fancy home, and he married Mama when they were very young, and then he realized his mistake—that she could never fit into his life, and he—"

"Oh, are you a nut!" Veronica sneered, but she kept looking at the picture, and feeling angry, and wondering what had really happened. Mama said only that they didn't get along together—and with all Mary Rose's sneaking around behind closed doors, and listening to whispered conversations, she had never found out why. But Mama had never cried again like she had that time on the subway. Veronica clenched her fists. And it had better not happen again.

Every Christmas a card arrived with some money in it, which Mama always took to buy clothes for them. Usually the card had only a short message on it, something like "Merry Christmas to my darling daughters, Veronica and Mary Rose, from your loving Papa." Last year he had sent presents instead of money—two mother of pearl crosses for them on silver chains.

"You know," Mary Rose said, looking hard at the picture. "I think I remember sitting on his lap, and him kissing me."

Veronica snorted. "You were only two when they broke up, so how could you remember him?"

"I do so remember him," Mary Rose said stubbornly. "I have a very good memory, a lot better than yours," she added spitefully.

Veronica could scarcely remember her Papa at all, aside from that time on the subway. She did remember a time at the zoo when she was very little. She was feeding peanuts to the elephant, and a big man was holding her. The elephant's trunk slithered toward her, and she turned and screamed, and buried her face in the man's jacket. It must have been her Papa who was holding her then, but when she tried to see the man's face in her mind, it was Ralph's face and not her Papa's.

Mary Rose jerked her head up suddenly. "Shh, someone's coming." She jumped up and slid the picture into the drawer, and had just closed it when Mama came into the room.

"We'll have to do some shopping," Mama said, and started to sit down on the chair. But yesterday's clothes were piled all over it, and she said angrily, "How many times do I have to tell you to put your dirty clothes in the hamper? This place looks like a pig sty." She looked like she was going to go on in the usual way, but she stopped and looked at them thoughtfully. "I guess you'd both better go for haircuts. Let's see, today is Wednesday. We'll go shopping tomorrow, and Friday, you can go to the barbershop and get your hair cut. Your father will be here Tuesday or Wednesday." She looked around the room. "Hmm, I guess we can put some clean curtains up here, and maybe I ought to put up something else on the living-room windows too. There's the rug, we can get down too." She shook her head wearily.

"Shopping?" Mary Rose reminded her.

"Yes. We'd better get some new clothes for the two of you. So many expenses this month, but we'll just have to manage. I'll take off a few hours from the store tomorrow, and we'll go down to Alexanders. Stanley can stay with Ralph at the store." She stood up, and then she said thoughtfully, "Maybe I'd better take the whole day off tomorrow, and straighten things up around here. I was supposed to finish that alteration on Mrs. Doyle's dress, but maybe I can work on that at home tomorrow night. Anyway, I'll meet you over at school. Don't forget. I'll be waiting outside the yard, and we'll go shopping right from there." She began walking out of the room. At the door she turned and shouted at them, "And put all those dirty things in the hamper."

After she was gone, Veronica began gathering up all the clothes from the chair, the floor, the top of the dresser. Mary Rose sat on the bed, hugging her legs and crowing, "New clothes for us, and it's not even Christmas."

4

Veronica was halfway to school the next morning when she remembered that she had forgotten about Peter Wedemeyer.

"I was going to wait for him, and beat him up on his way to school," she grumbled. "And today we're going shopping after school so I can't get him then."

"Well, that's all right," Mary Rose said comfortingly. "Give him a day. He'll think you forgot, and you'll be able to catch him easier tomorrow. He won't be suspicious."

Veronica nodded. She could be patient. What was the big hurry anyway? Whether it was going to be today or tomorrow, the outcome was certain.

He'd never mess with her again. Today he was probably shaking in his pants. Good! Let him shake a day longer. Serve him right.

In the schoolyard, Mary Rose faded away, and the last Veronica saw of her, she was following along after that drip Annette de Luca. Veronica moved along the inside of the school gate, noting how the children moved out of her way as she came. Not one of them would dare to start in with her, and once she got Peter settled, she could relax for a while—until a new kid arrived, anyway. In front of her, leaning against the gate, she saw Linda Jensen and Frieda Harris. They had their arms around each other's shoulders and were whispering and giggling into each other's ears. Funny how they'd been doing that ever since kindergarten. You'd think by now they'd have run out of things to say to each other. Veronica looked at them curiously, but then Frieda saw her, whispered something quickly to Linda, and pulled her away from the gate. They hurried off, leaving a clear path for Veronica, and she stood looking after them, and wondering what Frieda had said.

> *"Veronica Ganz*
> *Smells like cans*
> *Of fish."*

Caught off guard, Veronica whirled around sharply, and there was Peter, holding his nose and grinning at her. Bill Stover and Paul Curran were standing next to him, grinning too. But when they saw her looking at them, they both stopped grinning and pretended to be looking up at the sky. Peter, though, still holding his nose, began dancing around, singing,

> "*Down in the meadow in a itty bitty stream*
> *Swam three little fishies and a Mama fishie too.*
> *'Swim,' said the Mama fishie, 'Swim if you can*
> *Cause here comes Veronica*
> *Who'll give you a bam.'*"

What a stoop! Veronica thought in amazement. Her arms actually began aching, and her fingers curled in anticipation. She took a step or two toward him, saw Bill and Paul begin running, and then checked herself. The schoolyard was no place. Too many teachers around. And what she planned to do to Peter had to be done in the wide open spaces, without any nosy grownups. No, she'd wait! With an effort, she forced herself to turn around and move slowly away from him and the sound of his song, which he was obligingly singing over again.

She felt a little better as the lines began moving up the stairs. Snatching the hat off Rosalie Fry, in front of her, she playfully tossed it down the stairs to somewhere between the first and the second landing.

"My hat!" shrieked Rosalie.

"Who said that? Who talked on line?" the monitor on the second landing said, peering down over the sea of heads.

"Just playing a little game," Veronica crooned. "Wanna play?"

But when the monitor saw it was Veronica, she just acted like nothing had happened, and the lines continued upstairs.

Between the second and the third landing, Veronica bent down and pretended to tie her shoe. The whole line had to stop and wait for her.

"What's going on down there?" the monitor on the third landing shouted down. "What's holding up the line?"

"It's only little old me," Veronica said in a baby voice, sitting down on the step. "My laces are untied, and I don't know how to tie them."

"Oh!" said the monitor, and retreated to a safe corner of the landing.

As she passed the monitor on the fourth landing, Veronica began singing, "Anchors aweigh, my boys, anchors aweigh . . ." and tried to look in the girl's face. She even stuck her face up real close, but the monitor's eyes seemed intent on something in the distance.

Veronica's class 8B[4], was on the top floor of the building, and by the time the class arrived at its room, she had regained most of her usual good temper. The children sat down in their seats, and row by row, starting with the first row, they filed

into the clothes closet and hung up their coats.
Veronica had the last seat in the sixth row, near
the window. Peter Wedemeyer also sat in the sixth
row, but his seat was the first. He was already
seated when she started walking up the row, and he
held his nose and made a strangling noise as she
walked by.

It was too much. He was spoiling her day, that's
what he was doing. Veronica watched the lines
file in and out of the clothes closet. The first,
second, third, now the fourth. Maybe she could
just get a few quick but hard jabs in under the
darkness of the clothes closet. Just a little prelude
to tomorrow's action. That would make her feel a
lot better. As their line rose, and moved toward
the closet, Veronica hurried forward, elbowing several children in front of her out of the way. When
she entered the closet, she could see Peter over in
the left-hand corner and she started toward him.
But Peter just lowered his head and charged. "Oof,"
gasped Veronica, and Peter stepped delicately
through the door. Even though she whacked Paul
Lucas one, it wasn't the same, and when she emerged
into the light again, and saw the gentle smile on
Peter's lips and the innocent look in his blue eyes,
she knew she had to do *something* today or life
would not be worth living.

Miss Merritt, their teacher, was assigning jobs to
different children in the class.

"Linda Jensen, you may be the attendance monitor today. John Brody, I'd like you to empty the waste-paper basket. Uh—Veronica Ganz—could you please clean the board erasers this afternoon, and, Douglas Green, perhaps you can help."

Veronica nodded carelessly. Banging board erasers together outside in the schoolyard was one job she really didn't mind. But her partner usually did. Douglas Green, a soft, timid boy, would be a pleasant person to clean erasers on.

But then suddenly an idea burst into Veronica's mind, and she raised her hand, and leaped to her feet, and said, "Please, Miss Merritt, I cleaned the board erasers last week."

Miss Merritt looked at her nervously. Miss Merritt was so young and so nervous.

"Did you, Veronica? I didn't think you had."

"Oh yes, Miss Merritt, I did," Veronica insisted, crossing her fingers. "But I would love to water the plants. I never get to water the plants, and I love plants."

A deep, thoughtful silence penetrated the class-room.

"Why, Veronica," Miss Merritt said, flushing a little with pleasure, "I didn't realize you liked plants so much."

"Oh I do, I do," Veronica said passionately.

"Well in that case," Miss Merritt beamed, "why don't you water the plants, and perhaps if you do a good job—"

"Yes, ma'am," Veronica said, hurrying over to the watering can near the window sill.

"That's a good idea," Miss Merritt said enthusiastically. "Go ahead and water them right now." Miss Merritt smiled thoughtfully as Veronica hurried out of the room to fill up the can with water. She had always believed, in spite of what some of her older colleagues said, that there was really no such thing as a bad child. Just plumb the depths of that child's heart, and find what it was that interested him, and encourage him to develop that interest. For a while, it is true, she had wondered if there was anything that interested Veronica besides smacking other children. Funny how she had never thought of flowers. So often she had seen Veronica looking out of the window in what she had thought was boredom, while actually the child was probably looking at the rows of flowerpots that lined the sills, hungering for a chance to care for them. How foolish she had been! How insensitive! Miss Merritt's thoughts moved ahead to a bright and flower-laden future. She would encourage this interest in Veronica. She would appoint her permanent flower monitor, give her books on gardening, flower arrangement, maybe take her to a flower show. She continued talking to the class, but her mind followed gently along with that new Veronica who loved plants and found in their care a constructive way to express herself.

Veronica returned, and her face was aglow with eagerness. Miss Merritt was talking to the class about next week's trip to the Museum of Natural History, but her eyes followed Veronica as she moved from pot to pot, starting at the back of the room. Every so often Miss Merritt saw her hesitate and saw her eyes raised questioningly to hers, and each time Miss Merritt tried to nod encouragingly. Slowly, Veronica moved down the row of pots, and, with each pot watered, Miss Merritt saw another milestone in the renaissance of Veronica Ganz.

The last pot was watered. Miss Merritt turned for one moment to ask Jerome Kirschenbaum to be sure to bring in his permission slip from his mother for the trip when—a terrible howl, and Ralph Crespi was standing up, his hair plastered down on his head, and water dripping from every part of him.

"I tripped," Veronica cried, biting her lip angrily. And the terrible thing was that it was true. She had really tripped, and the water had missed its target, and gone spilling all over Ralph, who sat in the seat behind Peter.

"VerONICA . . ." began Miss Merritt.

"Yes, ma'am," said Veronica wearily, "I'm going." She put down the watering can and slunk out of the room on her way to the principal's office.

Later that afternoon, Veronica hurried across the schoolyard to where Mama stood right outside the gate. Mama was wearing her old wine-colored coat, but she had on her good black hat with the blue feathers, and she looked kind of pretty and excited. Mama didn't see her at first. She was looking at a boy in a brown jacket.

"My goodness," she said when she saw Veronica, "that's Mrs. Henderson's boy, Freddie. I haven't seen him in a long time. He's so big and nice-looking. I never would have recognized him." She looked at Veronica and sighed. "Time passes so quickly. No time at all I guess Stanley'll be like Freddie."

Veronica nodded, although she doubted that Stanley would ever look like Freddie Henderson, the best-looking boy in the whole school.

"Isn't that Rosalie Fry?" Mama asked. "She's in your class, isn't she?"

"Uh huh."

"Nice, polite, little girl," Mama said. "She opened the door in the grocery for me the other day."

Mama tried to catch Rosalie's eye, but Rosalie had hurried off with her eyes toward the ground as soon as she saw Veronica.

Mama looked after her thoughtfully. "Who else is in your class?" she asked. "I don't know any of your friends."

Friends! Veronica looked around helplessly. Paula Evans was coming slowly through the gate, but when she saw Veronica she began walking quickly. "Uh, that's Paula Evans. Hello, Paula." But Paula kept on walking.

"I guess she didn't hear you," Mama said.

Jeffrey Lobel approached them. "Hello, Jeffrey," Veronica said in a powerful voice. Jeffrey jumped, but he said, "Oh—hi, Veronica," and managed a weak smile as he hurried away.

"Handsome boy," Mama said, smiling, and looking after him.

"Hi, Rose Ellen," Veronica shouted. "Hi, Jimmy. Hi, Gladys . . ."

"Oh—hi, Veronica."

"Hello, Veronica."

"Hiya."

"What nice children," Mama said, nodding after their backs. "Looks like you know a lot of people this term."

"Hello, Jack . . . Vernon. . . . Hi, Cathy," Veronica bellowed, and Mama beamed and nodded as the children went by. She put an arm on Veronica's shoulder, and said, "I guess everything's going fine in school this term. Isn't it, Veronica?"

"Sure, Mama, sure," Veronica said quickly.

Mama sighed. "I knew you'd settle down sooner or later. You've got a good head on your shoulders, and whatever happens I want you and Mary Rose to finish school."

"That's right, Mama," Veronica said, looking away. There was a letter, addressed to Mama, inside her schoolbag. It was from the principal, Mr. Ferguson, and although Veronica hadn't seen what he had written, she was pretty sure it ended with an invitation for Mama to come and see him. Mama had been coming up to see Mr. Ferguson since second grade, and she'd gotten to know him pretty well. Veronica knew Mama would really give it to her when she saw the note. A note from Mr. Ferguson always meant two explosions. One when Mama read the note, and the other when she came home after talking to Mr. Ferguson.

And the awful thing was that it had all been for nothing anyway. If it had been Peter, instead of Ralph, standing there in the aisle, his mouth opening and closing like a fish's, it would have been worth a dozen notes from the principal and two dozen scenes with Mama. How could she have been so clumsy! She had been holding the can so carefully, and Peter's head was right in front of her, so close that she could see the little point that his hair made on the nape of his neck. Veronica clenched her fists. He'd been lucky, all right, but tomorrow—he wouldn't be so lucky tomorrow.

"And what did you do in school today?" said Mama.

"Look!" replied Veronica, grateful for the sudden vision of her sister, bounding across the yard, "there's Mary Rose. Let's go!"

5

Monday passed—Tuesday, Wednesday, Thursday.
There were clean curtains hanging in the girls' bedroom and in the living room. Mama had made Ralph
carry up the rug from the basement, and helped
him lay it on the living-room floor. The rug hadn't
been down for several years and there were moth holes
all over it, and many spots where it had faded.
Mama bit her lip when she saw it, and she made
Ralph roll it up again and take it back to the
basement. The torn window shade in the kitchen
had been replaced with a new one that looked much
whiter than the white of the old kitchen curtains.
So Mama took the curtains down and dyed them
green. They looked fine except for the band across

the edge that had been pink, and was now a strange color impossible to classify.

"No one's going to look that closely," Ralph said gently.

There were doilies all over the place. On the couch, the two chairs, the coffee table, the end tables, the radio cabinet. Mama even put a few extra ones on the back of the couch where the grease stains showed after all the jackets and papers had been removed.

"If anyone," Mama said over and over again, "throws anything on that couch or anywhere else in the living room, and if anyone forgets to hang up his or her clothes, or doesn't put her or his dirty underwear in the hamper, he or she will be *very* sorry."

On Monday there had even been a cleaning woman who came to wash the windows and wax the floors and scrub the woodwork. Stanley refused to go to school when she arrived in the morning, and Veronica and Mary Rose hurried home from school that afternoon to watch.

Mary Rose put on quite a performance for the cleaning woman, calling Mama "Mother," and generally trying to create the impression that she was a person who was used to having somebody clean her house. But the cleaning woman didn't even seem to see or hear them. She just kept on working, never even looked at them, and didn't bother to answer all the questions Stanley kept asking.

By Tuesday the house looked like somebody else's house. It even smelled like somebody else's house. Their new dresses hung in the closet—ready. They all had haircuts. Even Stanley and Ralph had haircuts, and Mama put polish on her fingernails.

They were certain there would be a letter on Tuesday. But there wasn't. Neither was there a letter on Wednesday nor on Thursday nor Friday. They hung around the whole day on Saturday, waiting, even though nothing came in the mail that day either. Sunday morning, Mary Rose started to cry, so Mama yelled at her, but then she gave them money and told them to go to the movies, and take Stanley. Ralph could always come and get them if they were wanted.

By Monday morning the house began looking and smelling as it always had. Mary Rose was taking it the hardest. She kept pulling out her new dress and trying it on. And Monday morning she put it on and said she was wearing it to school.

"No you are NOT!" Mama said, and Mary Rose grumbled and whined, but she had to go and change into her blue skirt and sweater just the same.

"I'll bet *she* wrote and told him not to come," Mary Rose said on the way to school. "*She* doesn't care for us. *She* just wants to ruin our lives."

"Oh cut it out," Veronica snapped. "*He's* not coming. That's all. *He* just changed his mind. *He's* the one who doesn't care for us, not her."

Mary Rose sniffed miserably.

"Anyway, who cares!" Veronica continued. "I've got other things to do besides sitting around waiting for him."

Her ears and various other parts of her body still smarted from what Mama had said and done to her after talking to Mr. Ferguson. If there was any more trouble, Mr. Ferguson had said, she would be suspended from school and would not graduate in February.

"I've got my own problems to worry about," said Veronica. The main problem being how to get Peter Wedemeyer, and how to get him away from school. Because angry as she was at Mama and at Mr. Ferguson, and at Peter, especially at Peter, she had no intention of letting that little rat keep her from graduating. The thought of spending another term in P.S. 63 was so unbearable that, difficult as it might be, Veronica had made up her mind to behave herself for the next three months—from November to February. More specifically, this meant that she would have to be careful in school. But only in school! Outside of school, she could do what she liked. Outside of school was no man's land, and even Mr. Ferguson could not pursue her beyond the boundaries of the schoolyard.

Peter Wedemeyer was turning into the biggest headache she'd ever had. True, she had been too busy last week to devote her full attention to him, but nevertheless she was beginning to feel that his powers of fading into thin air were almost magical. Last Wednesday morning, she had arrived on his block at eight-fifteen and hidden herself in the hallway of the house across the street, with a clear view of Peter's house. But somehow or other, Peter had never materialized. Probably he had seen her, although she certainly had not seen him, and had gotten to school by zigzagging through the backyards that stretched behind his house and all the other houses on the street. On Thursday, she tried a different tack, and posted herself outside the schoolyard at eight-fifteen. But somehow or other Peter again managed to get inside without her seeing him. Thursday and Friday afternoons, after dismissal, she had waited around in vain outside the school. But on both afternoons she had really been in a hurry to get home to see if there was anything in the mail.

Today it was going to be different. Her father was obviously not coming. There was going to be nothing in the mail again, as there had been nothing all of last week. She wasn't going to waste any more time sitting around waiting. Today was Peter Wedemeyer's day, and today she was going to settle his hash if it took all night.

And boy, had he been asking for it! Tacks on her seat just about every day now, a dead fish in her

coat pocket on Thursday, and, always, those mad-
dening jingles.

> *"Veronica Ganz*
> *Has ants in her pants."*
>
> *"Veronica Ganz*
> *She raves and rants."*
>
> *"Go to France*
> *Veronica Ganz."*

Every day there was a different one, and if it
wasn't for the fact that some other kids were chim-
ing in, she'd almost be curious to see how long he
could keep making up different jingles. But the sit-
uation was growing out of hand, and unless she
straightened him out soon, she'd have a mass
revolt on her hands. He was having a very bad
effect on the other children and there was a growing
wave of giggles, whispers, and defiant looks. After
today, though, with Peter properly initiated, the
restlessness would cease.

"I'm not going home today after school," Veronica
said to Mary Rose as they approached the schoolyard. "Today I'm going to get Peter Wedemeyer."

"But you can't," Mary Rose cried. "There's sure
to be a letter today."

"There's not going to be a letter," Veronica said,
"and you know there's not. You meet me after
school. Today I'm going to wait by the Franklin

Avenue exit, and you can stand on the corner and
see if you see him coming the other way."

"I'm going home," said Mary Rose.

"No, you're not!"

"Yes I am, and you can't stop me!"

They were just outside the schoolyard, and Veron-
ica tried to grab Mary Rose's arm to give her an
"Indian burn" until she agreed to come. But Mary
Rose broke away and fled to safety inside the yard.

Mary Rose did not meet her after school, and
Peter Wedemeyer did not emerge from the Franklin
Avenue exit as she had hoped. After all the other
kids had passed through the doors, and it was quite
clear that he had eluded her once more, Veronica
wended her way up the street where Peter lived
and paused thoughtfully outside his house. A little
boy was sitting on the outside steps playing with
marbles.

"Hey you," she said. "Do you know Peter Wedemeyer?"

"Uh huh."

"Do you know if he's home?" Veronica continued.
"I'm looking for him."

"No, he just went away." The little boy looked
at her thoughtfully. "Are you Stanley Petronski's
sister?"

"Yes, but where did Peter go?"

The boy grabbed his marbles and went scurrying
off down the street.

"Come back," Veronica shouted to him. "I just want to ask you something. Hey! You forgot one of your marbles."

She stooped down and picked it up. It was a cat's-eye, too. "Hey!" she shouted. "Come back."

But the little boy ran faster, and it was all she could do to stop herself from chasing after him and finding out what he'd been doing to Stanley. Her fist clenched over the marble. It felt cool and smooth. She picked it up between her fingers and held it up to the light. What a beaut! Grimly, she put it in her pocket. She'd give it to Stanley when she got home. He'd probably earned it.

Now she turned her attention to Peter again. So he wasn't home. Well, where was he? Would she have to spend her whole life chasing after him and never finding him? A powerful surge of helplessness grew inside her, and she sat down on the step and struggled against it. She just had to find him, and beat him up, and stop him from making fun of her. If she didn't, nobody else would, and for a moment a terrible feeling of loneliness and despair beat against the back of her eyes, and made her blink hard to stop from crying. But only for a moment. Because, all of a sudden, it came to her how easy it all was going to be—particularly since he wasn't home.

Up the stairs she strode, through the door, and knocked gently at the door marked 3A. The door opened. A woman who looked like a mother stood there. "Yes?" she said.

"Is Peter home?" said Veronica in a small, pleasant voice.

"No, he's not," said the mother.

"Oh," Veronica said, trying to look disappointed. "I needed to see him. Do you know where he is?"

"Are you Roslyn Gellert?" said Mrs. Wedemeyer, beginning to smile.

Veronica just smiled back. Imagine anybody taking her for Roslyn Gellert! But who knew where this might lead. And, besides, she didn't say she was.

"Peter told me there was a nice little girl in his class," Mrs. Wedemeyer said, blinking up at Veronica, "whom he'd been helping with her arithmetic problems. Are you having a little less trouble with them now, Roslyn?"

"Oh yes," Veronica said. "I'm really doing fine. I'm just sorry Peter isn't home because I . . . I had something to show him."

"Maybe I can help," Mrs. Wedemeyer said, opening the door wider.

"Oh no, ma'am, it has to be Peter."

Mrs. Wedemeyer said proudly, "He really does have a way of explaining things. It's not because he's my son. Everybody says so. Why, the other day, Mrs. Johnson in the rear apartment there"—Mrs. Wedemeyer stepped out into the hall to point the apartment out to Veronica—"wasn't able to turn off

the hot water faucet in her kitchen sink. Well, my Peter went in, and he figured it all out, and he . . ."

Veronica stood on one leg, impatiently listening to the whole long story Mrs. Wedemeyer had to tell about how Peter understood immediately what was wrong with the faucet, and how he had shown Mrs. Johnson how to fix it, and what Mrs. Johnson had to say about Peter. Then Mrs. Wedemeyer went on to tell how she had this recipe for sponge cake, but she didn't want to make the whole one, and half would not have been enough, and how Peter had worked out a two third's recipe that turned out just perfect.

"Mrs. Wedemeyer," Veronica cried desperately, "I just want to know where . . ."

But Mrs. Wedemeyer kept right on talking. She told Veronica how Peter had been on the honor roll for every single term in the old school where he used to go before he moved here, how his teachers were astonished by his scholarship, how neatly he folded up his clothes every night without anybody telling him, and how he always carried all the heavy bundles of laundry for her.

Mrs. Wedemeyer paused for a second to take a breath, and in that second Veronica said quickly, "Where is he?"

"At the library," Mrs. Wedemeyer answered, inhaling deeply, and continued telling Veronica how Peter read all the time—such books—way over the heads of most children his age—books even her husband would have trouble with.

"Well, yes, thank you very much, Mrs. Wedemeyer, "Veronica said, easing her way toward the outer door. "I'll see if I can catch—I mean find—him at the library."

"It's been very nice talking to you, Roslyn," Mrs. Wedemeyer said, "and if you see Peter, tell him to cross by the lights."

"Yes, ma'am, I'll tell him," Veronica leered. "G'bye."

She hurried down the steps, and practically flew up 169th Street to the library. She certainly would tell Peter to cross by the lights, she thought lightheartedly as she climbed the long flight of stairs to the children's room. While she was blackening both of his eyes, she'd tell him to be sure to cross by the lights.

Inside the room, Veronica passed the big desk, and paused to look around her warily. It had been a long, long time since she'd been to the library. Back in fifth grade, was it, the teacher had made them all get library cards, and she had taken out a book about horses or something, had lost the book, lost the card, and gotten all kinds of letters from the library saying how much money she owed, and how she couldn't take any more books out until she paid up.

Partially hidden by the crowd around the desk,

Veronica tried to locate Peter in the big room. Once she saw him, she'd just sneak away downstairs before he saw her, and wait until he came out. Then she'd deliver his mother's message, and deliver some other things as well. But there were so many children in the room, and several corners that she couldn't see into at all. So slowly, and quietly, she moved away from the desk and began to circle the room. Twice, she moved around it. Peter was not there.

Either he had come and gone while she'd been trailing him or, and she hoped this was the case, he had not yet arrived. Veronica sat herself down at a table and kept her eyes glued to the entrance.

"Now what was the name of that book?" she heard someone say. A librarian was leading a boy over to the catalog that stood near the table where Veronica sat.

"I think it's the *Little Captive Lad*," said the boy, and he watched as the librarian flipped through the cards in the catalog.

"Here it is," she said, "*Little Captive Lad*, and the author's last name is Dix. You'll find it over in the D's in the fiction section."

The boy thanked her, and was gone. A few minutes later, the librarian returned with a girl.

"It's three something or maybe it's four something. And it has a lot of good stories in it. My girl friend had it out last week."

"Three . . . three . . . three," hummed the librarian, flipping through the cards again. Veronica unfastened her eyes from the entrance and watched.

"Three . . . three . . ." said the librarian. "Here we are. *Three Boys and a Dog?*"

"No," said the girl.

"*Three Cats Go West?*"

"No."

"*Three Friends of Long Ago?*"

"No."

"*Three Golden Oranges?*"

"That's it, that's it," said the girl, nodding.

"The author's name is Boggs," said the librarian. "It's over in the fairy-tale section. Come along. I'll help you find it."

Veronica watched them walk off together. The librarian moved quickly to a certain shelf, pulled out a book, and handed it to the girl. Veronica began watching her in between keeping an eye on the door. Back and forth from the catalog to the bookshelves she went, finding books, and acting as if there wasn't any book in the whole place she didn't know. Such certainty! Such confidence in her own ability! Such assurance! Veronica took another look at the door, thought for a few minutes, grinned wickedly, and decided to have a little fun while she waited for Peter. The next time the librarian moved in her direction, Veronica stood up and said, "Uh, miss, could you help me find a book?"

"Why certainly," replied the librarian, her round face confident. "What's it called?"

"Well, I think it's called *The Mystery of the Hidden Shoes*."

"Mmm . . . mystery . . . mystery of . . ." said the librarian, flipping through the cards. Veronica stood patiently by her side. "*Mystery of the Hidden Door, Mystery of the Hidden Treasure, Mystery of the Hidden Villa*. I don't see anything listed called *The Mystery of the Hidden Shoes*. Are you sure you have it right?"

"Oh yes, ma'am," Veronica said, taking a quick peek at the entrance. "I think the author's name is Toes."

"Toes?" said the librarian. "How do you spell it?"

"T-O-Z-E," said Veronica carefully.

"That's an odd name," said the librarian, but she began looking through the cards in the T drawer.

"I think it's I. C. Toze," Veronica said, and waited. The librarian continued flipping the cards unsuspectingly, and said finally that they just did not have that book in the library.

"There's another one I'd like then," Veronica said.

"Good," said the librarian kindly. "Maybe we can find that one for you."

"It's called *The Crazy Man*."

"I see," said the librarian. But this time she did not begin flipping through the cards. "And the author? Do you know his name?"

"Yes, ma'am," said Veronica with a serious face. "It's U. R. Looney."

The librarian just cocked her head to one side, and looked at Veronica. "I don't think," she said crisply, "that you are really in a mood for books today. Why don't you run along now, and come back another day."

"Yes, ma'am," Veronica said agreeably, "but there is another book I wanted. It's called—"

"Another day," said the librarian emphatically. "Good-bye."

Veronica leaped down the stairs chuckling to herself. Now that had been fun, and she certainly would return on another day.

A couple of hours later, after canvassing the park, Peter's block, the schoolyard, and several other likely spots, Veronica returned home. She hadn't found Peter after all, but in the park she had found a tennis racket without a handle and a slightly rusted flashlight that should work once she got some new batteries for it. Her new possessions, particularly the flashlight, made her feel that the day had not been completely wasted.

As she opened the door to the apartment, Mary Rose came running out of the living room, her cheeks flushed, a letter in her hand.

"Veronica," she cried, "see, it's from Papa. He didn't forget. Something came up in his business, and he couldn't leave. In a few weeks, he says. For sure by Christmas."

6

"Mademoiselle Fry," said Madame Nusinoff, "*levez-vous.*"

Rosalie stood.

"*J'ai vingt-et-un fleurs dans mon jardin,*" said the teacher, "*et vous avez quinze fleurs dans votre jardin. Qui a plus de fleurs?*"

Rosalie blinked. A nervous silence enveloped the rest of the class as each child went over in his mind the teacher's question, and what the appropriate answer should be. Veronica watched the mole over Madame Nusinoff's lip twitch.

"*Avez-vous étudié la leçon,* Mademoiselle Fry?" inquired Madame Nusinoff politely.

"Yes I have but—"

"*En français*," commanded the teacher.

"*Oui*."

"*Eh bien—quelle est la réponse?*"

Rosalie bit her lip and looked up at the ceiling. "*Asseyez-vous!*" said Madame Nusinoff, putting a mark in the book on her desk. Rosalie sat down. The teacher's eyes swept over the classroom and rested on Paul Curran. "*Monsieur Curran*," she said, "*levez-vous, s'il vous plaît*."

Paul cast one last desperate look at the open book on his desk, and very slowly stood up.

"*Monsieur Curran*," said Madame Nuisnoff, "*j'ai vingt-et-un fleurs dans mon jardin, et vous avez quinze fleurs dans votre jardin. Qui a plus de fleurs?*"

Paul hesitated, and then said without very much conviction, "*Moi . . .*"

"*Pourquoi?*"

Paul took a deep breath. "*Parce que vous avez . . .*" His vocal chords failing him, Paul's hands began describing larger and larger arcs in the air. The mole on Madame Nusinoff's upper lip twitched once again, and Veronica burst out laughing.

"*Asseyez-vous*, Monsieur Curran," said Madame Nusinoff, putting another mark in the book on her desk. Then she looked at Veronica.

"Mademoiselle Ganz," she said, "*levez-vous, s'il vous plaît*."

Veronica rose, and leaned, smiling against her desk.

The teacher droned again, "*J'ai vingt-et-un fleurs dans mon jardin, et vous avez quinze fleurs dans votre jardin. Qui a plus de fleurs?* Mademoiselle Ganz, *traduisez la question, s'il vous plaît.*"

"You said," Veronica answered, "that you have twenty-one flowers in your garden, and that I have fifteen flowers in my garden. Who has more flowers?"

"*Bon!*" said Madame Nusinoff. "*Et la réponse?*"

"*Vous,*" said Veronica, grinning.

"*Bon! Et pourquoi?*"

"Because," said Veronica, the grin stretching all over her face, "I don't have a garden."

There was a general sucking in of breaths from all corners of the classroom, quickly followed by a rising wave of titters.

The mole twitched again, but Madame Nusinoff just said tonelessly, as if nothing unusual had been said, "*En français.*"

Feeling a little foolish, Veronica said, "*Parce que je n'ai pas un jardin.*"

"*Asseyez-vous,* Mademoiselle Ganz," said the teacher, "*et restez ici après la classe!*"

Then Madame Nusinoff proceeded, in French, to tell the class that it was obvious that most of them had not done the homework, that many of them were sure to fail French, and that they must also be going to fail math if they couldn't answer a simple question in subtraction such as the one she had presented to them. Her specific comments were not completely understood by most of the students, who were delighted to have her talking anyway and were only hoping that she would continue berating them in French or any other language she chose until the bell rang. Unfortunately, with about fifteen minutes to go, Madame Nusinoff resumed the inquisition, and it was not until Peter Wedemeyer was called upon that the question was finally answered to her satisfaction.

Then Madame Nusinoff, in English this time, told the class that the French Club, of which she was the faculty advisor, was going to put on a pageant for Christmas—in French of course. It would include French songs, French dances, and a play. More actors were needed, and she asked if there were any children in the class who would like to join the club and take part in the pageant. Peter's hand immediately shot up. Madame Nusinoff wrote his name down in her book, and looked around the classroom with one eyebrow raised. Linda Jensen put up her hand, so naturally Frieda Harris raised hers too. Then very slowly the hands of Reba Fleming, Frank Scacalossi, and Lorraine Jacobs floated upward. Madame Nusinoff wrote. Just as the bell rang, Paul Curran's right hand, which had been held tightly under his desk by his left hand, broke free and jerked up. Madame Nusinoff's eyebrow rose a little higher, but Paul's name was duly recorded.

"We will meet Friday afternoon at three-thirty in the auditorium," said Madame Nusinoff. "If anyone else decides to join us, meet us then."

Veronica ambled over to the desk, and stood looking out into the hall, and tapping one foot in rhythm to bop de dum dum, dum dum. The teacher had told her to remain after class, and that's what she was doing. She knew that Madame Nusinoff would just tell her off, read her the riot act, and send her on her way, as she had done so many times before. Madame Nusinoff, for all her grumpiness, never sent people to the principal, which was one reason why she liked Madame Nusinoff better than most of her other teachers.

Paul Curran stopped by the desk, too, and began explaining to Madame Nusinoff that he really had known the correct answer to her question about the flowers in the garden but that he had been thrown by translating "I" and "you." She had said in French "I have twenty-one flowers in my garden and you have fifteen flowers." But when he translated it in his own mind, he became the "I" and she the "you." So that was why he wasn't sure who had the six extra flowers, although he realized one of them had.

"I see," said Madame Nusinoff frostily.

Paul looked meaningfully at the record book on her desk, but since she made no move in its direction, he said sadly, "Good morning," and moved off.

"Veronica," said Madame Nusinoff when they were alone, "you were very funny today."

Veronica looked away modestly.

"Very funny," continued Madame Nusinoff. "Now I hope you're going to think it's funny when I tell you that you'll probably fail French on the next report card period."

Veronica looked slyly at Madame Nusinoff. She really didn't think she was going to fail. Madame Nusinoff had threatened this before, but French was the one subject she seemed to do well in.

"You knew the right answer to the question," Madame Nusinoff said impatiently. "Why didn't you give it?"

Veronica shrugged.

"I wouldn't be surprised if you even did the homework last night," continued Madame Nusinoff.

"I did not," Veronica said, shocked.

Madame Nusinoff laughed. "You see," she said, "you didn't even do the homework, and yet you knew the right answer. Just think how much you'd really know if you studied."

"Sometimes I do the homework," Veronica said grudgingly.

"I know you do—a lot more often than you want people to know. And I'll tell you something, Veronica, if you did your work, you could be a very good student in French. You really like it, don't you?"

As a matter of fact, although she certainly wasn't going to admit it to the teacher, she did like French, very much in fact. Being able to say words in another language made her feel powerful and important. Sometimes when Mary Rose wasn't around, she'd close the door to their bedroom, stand in front of the mirror, and speak to her reflection in French.

"It's all right," she said.

"With a little time and effort," the teacher said persuasively, "you could be a very good student, maybe even as good as Peter Wedemeyer."

"That little runt," Veronica said scornfully.

"Yes, he is a little runt, isn't he?" Madame Nusinoff said thoughtfully. "I'd forgotten how small he was. You know, Veronica, you and Peter have something in common, don't you?"

"What!"

"Your size. You're taller than everybody else, and he's smaller. Maybe it makes you both feel different sometimes from other people. But Peter doesn't let his size stop him. He doesn't feel he has to be funny all the time, or mean to make up for his size. He's too smart to let it stop him. And nobody notices after a while how small he is. They see other things about him—important things—and they respect him and like him."

"I hate him," Veronica said between her teeth.

"Why?"

"Because he makes fun of me all the time. He sings funny songs about me, and he laughs at me, and . . . and . . . he threw old fish bones all over me."

"Peter Wedemeyer!" said Madame Nusinoff. "I can't believe that."

"No," said Veronica savagely, "nobody believes it. Because it's not the same thing being smaller than everybody else. It's easier being smaller. People are always sorry for you when you're small but when you're big like me . . ."

Madame Nusinoff stood up, and put an arm on Veronica's shoulder. "I'm sorry for you, Veronica," she said.

Madame Nusinoff's mole had two little hairs in it. Veronica had never realized that before. She had never stood so close to Madame Nusinoff before. It was a terrible thing standing so close to a person who was a teacher that you could see those two hairs, and feel so much like crying.

"Leave me alone," she shouted. "You don't have to be sorry for me. Just leave me alone." She broke away from that arm on her shoulder and ran out of the room.

Hurrying along the hall, she thought how much she hated Madame Nusinoff, how much she hated everybody. There was nobody you could trust. Up until today she had kind of liked Madame Nusinoff, kind of enjoyed the French class, too, but here was Madame Nusinoff tormenting her like everybody else. Oh, she couldn't wait to get out of this school! If it wasn't for that, she'd get even with Madame Nusinoff. She'd tear up all those papers on her desk, and write dirty words in that precious book of hers. She'd wait for her after school and throw rocks at her. The possibilities for revenge were end-less, and maybe after she graduated, she could come back one day and fix Madame Nusinoff real good. This was a comforting thought, and Veronica felt a little easier when she reached her home room. But the class wasn't there. She'd forgotten that they'd be down in the yard for recess. Good! She was really in the mood for punch ball. Veronica dropped her books on her desk, grabbed her coat, and hurried downstairs.

The children had already divided up into two teams for punch ball when she arrived. Today Peter was the captain of one team, and Harvey Douglas of the other. Miss Merritt told her to join Peter's team since he had one less than Harvey. Peter had never been captain before, and as she walked toward the team she could hear his excited voice saying, "Oh, we're going to win! We've got the best players on our team." When he saw Veronica approach, he said, "Hey! Are you going to be on our team too?"

"Wasn't my idea," Veronica said shortly. "Miss Merritt said I had to."

"Oh great," Peter said. "Now we'll really murder them."

Veronica acted unconcerned. People always wanted her on their teams.

"Now I'll take first base," Peter said, "Jeffrey can take second, Helen third, Veronica can be catcher, and Bertha, you be pitcher."

"I'll be pitcher," Veronica corrected. Lots of kids, she knew, liked to pitch, but that was her position, and whenever she played on a team, it was always understood that she would pitch.

"You're a good pitcher," Peter said agreeably, "but I think you'd make a better catcher."

"I'm pitching," Veronica insisted.

"Look," said Peter patiently, "I've been kind of studying the way everybody plays. Now Bertha here, she's sort of a dark horse. Nobody realizes that she's got a great curve ball."

"Who, me?" said Bertha, her fat cheeks turning red.

"Yes. You pitched last week on Gloria's team, and day before yesterday you pitched when Gerald fell down, and you've really got a wicked ball there. I've been watching you, and I think you've really got possibilities."

"Gee!" said Bertha.

"I'm pitching," said Veronica.

"Look," Peter said, "how do you know you won't like being a catcher unless you try? You're a good catcher. I've been studying the way you play, and you're kind of a solid fielder—but not too fast—and when you pitch, your balls are a little slow."

"You're full of baloney," Veronica shouted. "And if I don't pitch, I don't play."

"Well," said Peter, shrugging his shoulders, "Bertha's pitching, and you're just being a bad sport. Look—"

"Drop dead!" Veronica said. "I quit."

She walked away from the team, and leaned against the fence. Miss Merritt hurried over. "What's the matter, Veronica?" she said nervously. "What happened?"

"I'm not playing," Veronica said.

"But what happened, dear?" said Miss Merritt soothingly.

"I won't play on *his* team."

Miss Merritt sighed. She told Jack Tar, who was on Harvey's team, to go over to Peter's team, and she told Veronica to play on Harvey's team.

"I'm pitching," Veronica said when she joined her new team.

"Sure Veronica, sure," said Harvey.

Peter's team won 4 to 0.

After the game, Veronica overheard a conversation between a triumphant Peter and a radiant Bertha.

"What you have to work on now," Peter was saying, "is to pitch the ball in lower. Then nobody, but nobody, could connect."

"Gee," said Bertha, "I didn't even know I was so good."

"You know what?" Peter said. "How about meeting me this afternoon over at the park—that field outside the tennis court is a good place. We can work on developing your ball."

Bertha giggled, and agreed to be there at four.

Veronica whistled contentedly as she climbed the stairs to her classroom. And later, when the children

were playing in the yard after lunch, and Peter
began chanting

> *"Learn to dance*
> *Veronica Ganz.*
> *Because when you pitch*
> *You look like a witch"*

she could even find it in her heart to smile comfortably to herself. Because he might not be aware
of it at the moment, but she would settle the score
between them this afternoon at four in the field outside the tennis court.

7

"Go home, Stanley!" Veronica shouted over her shoulder.

Stanley stopped walking, and stood sideways, ready to run should she decide to give chase.

"Listen, Stanley," Veronica shouted, "you can't come today. That's all there is to it! Go home, and tomorrow I'll take you with me to . . . to the library."

"The library!" Stanley said, wrinkling up his face.

"Go home!"

"No."

Veronica made a few running jumps in his direction, and Stanley scurried off down the block. Veronica turned, ran around the corner, up the stairs of the first house she came to, and hid in the small vestibule, behind the glass doors. Sure enough, a few minutes later, there came Stanley trotting around the corner. Veronica pressed herself against the wall. Stanley did not see her and continued on his way down the street. As soon as he had passed, Veronica tried to open the inner door that led to the apartments but it was one of those doors that opened only if a tenant inside the building pressed a buzzer. Veronica inspected the mailboxes with the buttons under them, and selected F. MANCIE-WITZ—5E. That would be up on the top floor of the building. She pressed the button, and after a minute or so the buzzer buzzed, and Veronica opened the door and ran inside. At the back of the long hall was a staircase leading down to the yard.

"Who's there?" somebody shouted from way up the stairwell.

Down the stairs Veronica hurried, and tried the door to the yard.

"Is that you, Jacky?"

The door opened, and Veronica ran out into the yard. Good! It was the kind of yard that connected with all the others. She had to climb a stone wall, squeeze under a fence, and cut across several other yards, but she came out on Franklin Avenue, which led into the park also. It was quite a bit out of the way, but anything was better than having Stanley along when she was going to be involved in a fight.

Stanley was no good at all when it came to fighting. Mary Rose at least could be counted on to warn her if any grownups were coming. But Stanley would only stand there hiccuping and yelling, "Help! Help! They're killing Veronica." Which was ridiculous, of course, but also distracting.

Stanley was nowhere in sight when she reached the park. She cut across the bicycle path, jumped over the benches, and hurried along a path that led to the tennis courts. Nobody called her. Nobody made any noise. Nothing dropped. But the warning light flashed in Veronica's mind, and she knew she was being followed. She turned sharply. Stanley was just bending over, picking up a leaf, about twenty feet behind her.

"Look at this one, Veronica," he said happily, holding up a deep red leaf that stood away crisply from his hand.

"Stanley, I'm going to break your neck!" Veronica shrieked. "If I get my hands on you, you won't even know what hit you."

"Aw, Veronica, don't be like that," Stanley said, but he let the leaf go, turned sideways again, and stood poised for flight.

"For the last time, will you go home?" Veronica thundered.

"No."

"O.K. for you," said Veronica, with a meaningful shake of her fist. "I'll get you later, and boy will you be sorry."

She turned away from him and began running
along the path. What a pest! She didn't have the
time now, but later, after she finished with Peter,
she'd attend to Stanley. He'd been getting away
with murder lately, but this was the end. She'd fix
him so that he'd never follow her again.

Over the hill, there were the tennis courts. She
circled them quickly and paused, gasping for breath,
behind the privet hedge that led down to the big
field where Peter and Bertha had arranged to meet.
Carefully, she parted the bushes and peered down
the slope to the field. Yes, there they were, throwing
the ball back and forth. But her breath was coming
too fast to attempt any charge just at the moment.
She sat down in the path and tried to catch her
breath, and get rid of that dizzy feeling in her head.

Behind her in the tennis court there was a couple
dressed in white shorts and white shirts playing
tennis. *Pong* went the ball, *pong,* then *pong* again.
Stanley came slowly around the corner, saw her
sitting there, and moved off to a small slope on one
side of the tennis court. There were several tall
trees on the slope, and the ground was covered
with dead leaves. Stanley began walking through
the leaves. *Grunch, grunch, grunch,* went the sound
of Stanley walking through the leaves.

Through a space in the hedge Veronica could
see Bertha and Peter throwing the ball back and
forth. She couldn't hear them, but she could see
them, and suddenly Peter began jumping up and

down, up and down, clapping his hands. The agonizing shortness of breath was gone from her throat, and the sun on her head felt good. It was so warm and good sitting there in the path, hearing the *pong, pong* behind her, and Stanley's *grunch, grunch* from the slope, and seeing little Peter Wedemeyer jumping up and down, up and down.

Suppose now, just suppose, because that's not what she had in mind, but suppose anyway she were to get up and walk very slowly and carefully down the field, maybe with a smile to show that she wasn't sore—just supposing she wanted to, which she didn't—kind of acting like she just happened to be out walking and just happened to come across them there playing ball. And suppose Bertha—she didn't really have anything against Bertha. That was a long time ago when she tripped her on the stairs, and sat down on her soft rump. Veronica couldn't help smiling when she remembered how Bertha had squealed like a little pig—looked up and said, "Hi, Veronica." Well just supposing she said, "Hi, Bertha." What then? Maybe Peter might say, "Hey, you want to catch?" Just supposing he did. Well now, he wouldn't and she was going to beat him up today, wasn't she? She wanted to beat him up today. She'd gone to a lot of trouble to arrange for this opportunity, but just supposing he said it.

Peter and Bertha were throwing the ball back and forth again. *Pong* from the tennis players behind her, *grunch* from Stanley. Her happiness became almost unbearable. Just supposing now . . .

Carefully, she stood up, and slowly walked around the hedge to the opening that led down to the field. She smiled, and pretended to be looking up at the sky as she started walking toward them. Bertha saw her first. "There's Veronica," she shouted. "Run! Run!"

For such a fat girl, Bertha could run very fast. Dazed, Veronica watched her speeding away as if the cameras had suddenly doubled her normal speed. Then she looked at Peter. He was grinning at her, but as she began moving slowly toward him, he stuck out his tongue and started running.

When somebody starts to run away from you, the only thing you can do is run after him. Peter had a head start, and made good use of it. Up the hill, past the tennis courts, around Indian Lake, Peter ran, with Veronica after him.

Peter paused at the entrance to the playground, looked over his shoulder at Veronica, and began walking slowly toward a building right in the middle of the playground. Veronica raced through the entrance, saw Peter wave a hand in greeting, and then stroll nonchalantly into the side of the building marked BOYS.

Veronica shook her head. What a character that Peter was! Very, very clever of him, wasn't it, to take refuge in a place that she couldn't possibly enter. However—Veronica leaned comfortably against the front of the building—she had plenty of time this afternoon. And sooner or later, he'd have to come out, and there she'd be.

After a while, Stanley came hurrying into the playground. He didn't say a word to her, but just raced into the boy's room. When he came out, he had a thoughtful look on his face.

"Veronica," he said, "who's that boy in there?"

"Never mind," snapped Veronica, "and get away from here!"

"Veronica," Stanley said, "that boy asked me if there was a mean-looking girl standing outside, and I said, 'No, just my sister.' So he said who was my sister, and I said you. Then he said. 'Poor kid!' Why did he say poor kid, Veronica?"

"Never mind, Stanley," Veronica said sweetly. Nobody had to feel sorry for Stanley. "Go and play!"

"Are you going to stay here for a while?" Stanley said, looking anxiously toward the swings.

"Oh, yeah! I'll be here for a while."

"Well, O.K. then," Stanley said, walking toward the swings. "But don't go away."

"Stanley!" Veronica shouted after him.

"What?"

"Tie your shoelaces!"

"O.K."

"And Stanley!"

"What?"

"Wipe your nose!"

Stanley wiped his nose on his sleeve, and then climbed onto an empty swing.

"Come and push me, Veronica," he shouted.

"I can't."

"Why not?"

"I'm busy."

"What are you doing?"

"I'm just busy."

Stanley flung his body backward and forward on the swing, but he couldn't really raise himself very high. So he lay down on the swing, with his head dropping down on one side and his feet on the other. After a while he sat sideways in the swing, and pushed himself to and fro sideways until the kids on either side of him told him to stop.

Then he went over to the slide. The first time he went down just sitting with his legs out in front of him. The next time he went down feet first but lying on his back, then lying on his stomach head first, then feet first.

Veronica began walking back and forth in front of the building. Poor Peter, she thought almost affectionately, this is really the end of the line for him.

Next time she looked, Stanley was on the seesaw, sharing one end with another little boy about his size while a bigger, older boy was trying to balance on the other end. It didn't work. The two small boys together weighed less than the one big boy so their end whizzed high in the air, bumping them into loud delirious giggles. But they couldn't get his end up very high. After a while, each small boy took a different end while the bigger boy balanced in the center. That worked much better.

It grew darker, and Veronica reflected that at five the playground would close, and Peter would have to come out. Would he tell the playground attendant about her, she wondered. He might, and perhaps it would be smarter waiting for him outside the playground. He could come out only one entrance, and if she waited behind one of the bushes right outside, that might be the most sensible plan.

Stanley was sitting in the middle of the monkey bars, looking up at the top. Funny how scared he was about climbing to the top. Why when she was his age she could climb over a schoolyard fence.

"Go on, Stanley," she shouted, "climb up! It's great at the top."

"Hold me," Stanley suggested.

"I can't."

"Why not?"

"I'm busy."

"What are you doing?"

"Look, Stanley, if you're not going to climb to the top, come on down, and we'll go HOME." She said this in a very loud voice, hoping Peter would hear her, and be deceived about her intentions. "I'm going HOME NOW," she shouted.

Stanley climbed down and began heading toward her.

"Is your name Veronica?" asked a boy, coming over to her.

"Yeah?"

"Here!" The boy handed her a paper. "I met a kid down near the lake who said you'd be standing here, and to give you this."

Veronica looked down at the paper in her hand. It was a paper towel, and there was something written on it. Veronica held it up close to her face because it was growing almost too dark to see. The message was,

> *You don't have a chance*
> *Veronica Ganz.*
> > > *Peter W.*

"What did he look like?" she shouted at the boy.

The boy backed away. "I dunno," he said nervously. "Just looked like a boy."

"Was he short? Shorter than you?"

The boy nodded.

"Did he have a plaid jacket on?"

"I guess so." The messenger began walking away. "He just asked me if I was going to the playground, and said you'd be standing near the boy's room. That's all."

"*STANLEY!*" Veronica roared.

Stanley was standing right next to her. "What?"

"Go in there, and see if that boy is still inside."

Stanley walked into the boy's room, and quickly returned. "Nobody's in there," he said.

Veronica thought for a moment. "Stanley," she said, "is there a window in there?"

"Uh huh."

"Is it open?"

"I don't know. Should I look, Veronica?"

"Look!"

Stanley looked. "It's open," he said, "up to the top. Will you push me on the swing now, Veronica?"

"No!"

"Why not?"

"Because I'm busy."

"What are you doing?"

"I'm thinking!" Veronica shouted.

"Oh," Stanley said, "that's what you've been busy doing all day—thinking."

But Stanley was mistaken. Veronica had not been thinking all day, but now she was, and her mind creaked and groaned under its burden. Stanley stood looking up at her tormented face. "Veronica," he whimpered, "let's go home, Veronica."

But Veronica didn't hear him. She was fighting a hard battle now, and her adversary was herself. Peter Wedemeyer had eluded her and outfoxed her down the line. It wasn't enough that she was stronger than he. If she couldn't outsmart him, the victory would be his. She was going to need a new weapon to beat Peter, and that weapon lay somewhere inside her own brain. If she couldn't find it, then it was all over for her, and Peter could go on teasing and tormenting her forever and ever, and she'd never be

able to stop him. Was there any point in going on with this contest, which served only to humiliate her time and again? Should she admit that Peter was just too much for her—too smart for her? Should she forget the whole business, and keep out of his way? Or should she try again?

"I'm cold," Stanley whimpered. "I want to go home."

"In a minute, in a minute," she muttered, because there was something bursting into light inside her brain. A trap. Of course. A trap. She'd lay a trap. She'd beat him at his own game, and show him that she was as good as he, and twice as smart. She'd lay a trap for him that he'd walk right into. And how easy it all would be!

"Come on, Stanley," she said, taking his hand. "We'll go home now."

A few details would have to be worked out, but Veronica thought triumphantly as they hurried along through the park that this time she'd get him for sure. The web was spun, and she'd begin tightening the threads in the French Club on Friday afternoon.

8

"But he says so in the letter," Mary Rose insisted.

Mama began pouring the hot water from the tea-kettle over her feet in the basin.

"Listen," Mary Rose continued. "Right here it says." And she began reading. The letter really belonged to Mama since it had been addressed to her, but Mary Rose had appropriated it, and was keeping it with Papa's picture. "'Too bad it didn't work out, but tell the girls I'll be in New York for sure around Christmas.'"

"Aah," said Mama, handing the kettle back to Veronica, and arching her feet luxuriously in the steaming water.

"So why do you say he's not coming?"

"I did not say he wasn't coming," Mama said mildly. "I only said *if* he comes, and *if* doesn't mean he's not coming. I hope he is able to come, but *if* he doesn't, I don't want you to be disappointed."

"But he says right here he's coming, but you keep on saying *if*. Why should you say *if* when he says he's coming. Right here he says it. 'Tell the girls I'll be—'"

"I know, I know," Mama said, raising one flushed foot above the steam and allowing the other the freedom of the entire basin. "You've just read it out loud. I heard you the first time."

"So why do you keep saying *if?*" Mary Rose said angrily.

"Look, Mary Rose," Mama said, "all I want to do is soak my feet in peace. Please, be a good girl, and go away."

Mary Rose burst into tears. "I hate you," she cried. "I hate you. You spoil everything!"

Mama stood up and began climbing out of the basin, and Mary Rose ran, shrieking, out of the kitchen. Mama sat down again. "I don't know," she said, shaking her head. "I just don't know what to do about that child. She was always a problem, always gave me more trouble than anybody else. But lately she's just impossible." Mama's face looked troubled. "I just hope he comes this time."

Veronica handed Mama some more newspapers to lay down around the basin where it splashed when she stood up. "Don't you think he'll come?" she said

curiously. For her own part she didn't really care
so much whether he came or not. She had more
important things on her mind.

"Well, it's not the first time he said he was coming,"
Mama said tensely. She shook her head again. "I
wish you hadn't seen the letter. It's not fair for
the two of you to get all excited."

"I'm not excited," Veronica said coolly. "If he
doesn't want to come, he doesn't have to."

"Oh, I'm sure he wants to come," Mama protested.
"Don't go thinking he doesn't want to come, Veronica.
After all, he hasn't seen you since you were babies.
But you know how it is—he's so far away, and it
costs a lot of money, and—"

"And you don't believe he's coming?"

"Well," Mama said weakly, "let's hope he is. He
means well. He always did. But . . . here, Veronica,
hand me the kettle again. The water's cool."

Veronica handed her mother the kettle, and
watched the steam rise again from the basin.

"Mmm, that feels good," Mama said, leaning back
in the chair. "All day long I've been looking forward
to this."

"Be back in a minute," Veronica said. She walked
out of the kitchen and into the living room, where
Stanley sat at the window, looking out. He was
singing very softly and slowly, over and over again,
"purplemountedmajesties," and did not seem to hear
her as she passed through the room.

Mary Rose was crying in front of the mirror. She was just standing there, watching two spent-up tears disintegrating near her chin, and trying to force some more tears out from between her lids.

"The face on the bathroom floor," Veronica remarked pleasantly.

That helped. Two big lustrous tears sped naturally down her cheeks, and Mary Rose, watching them, sobbed, "Leave me alone! Leave me alone!"

Veronica shrugged, and began looking for her French book.

"What are you doing?" Mary Rose whimpered.

"What do you care?" said Veronica. "You said leave you alone so I'm leaving you alone. Now you leave me alone."

She picked up the book, walked to the door, and caught a glimpse of Mary Rose's face as she turned to leave. Mary Rose's face drooped, from the eyes down, in a funny way. Mary Rose cried a lot, but this time her face looked different, and something twisted inside Veronica's chest.

"Whatsamatter, Mary Rose?" she said helplessly.

Mary Rose broke out into fresh sobs and threw herself across the bed.

Veronica hesitated for a second, but then came back into the room, sat down on the bed, and began patting her sister's back.

"Aw, come on, Mary Rose, you'll make yourself buggy if you go on like that."

"He's got to come," Mary Rose sobbed into the bedclothes. "He's just got to come."

"Well, why should you care so much whether he comes or not?"

"Because I don't want to stay here any more," Mary Rose said, sitting up. "I hate it here. I want to go back to Nevada with him."

"How do you know he wants to take you back with him?"

"He does, he does. I know he does," Mary Rose said fiercely. "Sure he does. He always did, I bet, but *she* wouldn't let him. And it's not because she cares for us. You know she only cares for Stanley. It's just spite."

"You're really a nut," Veronica said crisply. "Why don't you leave her alone?"

"Sure, you always take her part," Mary Rose hissed, "but she doesn't like you any better than she likes me."

"Oh cut it out," Veronica said impatiently.

"Look at this room!" Mary Rose whined.

Veronica looked. "What's the matter with it?"

"This old bed, that old dresser, that old mirror—everything's old. Nothing's pretty."

She jumped up from the bed, grabbed a magazine that lay on the dresser, flipped through the pages, and practically threw it into Veronica's lap. "Look at that!" she said, accusingly.

There was a picture in the magazine of two girls about their own age. Both girls had long hair with ribbons in it, and both wore short plaid skirts and bright-colored knee socks that matched their sweaters. The older girl was standing up, reading a book, and the younger one lay stretched out on a fluffy, white rug, eating an apple and looking through an album of photographs. There were two beds in the room with fluffy pink bedspreads, and each bed had a canopy over it, covered with the same kind of ruffly pink material. There were two desks painted white, with two matching white chairs, and each desk had a lamp with a dainty pink shade. There was also a dressing table draped with deep rose-colored flounces, and topped by a heart-shaped mirror. The room had other pieces of furniture, too, all in pink and white.

Veronica looked at the picture, and then read the printing under it. "Feminine but Functional" it said, and went on to explain that even in cases where two girls had to share the same room, it was possible to make that room attractive, comfortable, and by careful attention to separation of room areas, privacy could also be assured.

Mary Rose looked at the picture over Veronica's shoulder. "Isn't it gorgeous?" she murmured.

"Uh huh," Veronica agreed, "but you have to be rich to have a room like that."

Mary Rose sat down on the bed next to Veronica. "Well, Papa has a lot of money. He's rich, and if we lived with him we could have a room like that. Maybe we could even have our own rooms." She pulled the magazine away from Veronica and studied the picture critically.

"It's beautiful," she said thoughtfully, "but I'm not sure pink is my color. Veronica, do you remember at the World's Fair, that home-decorating pavilion?"

"No," said Veronica.

"Well they gave out color charts to go with your personality. Wait, I'll show you."

Mary Rose had her papers and samples arranged in boxes stacked in the closet. She pulled out one box that was marked HOME DECORATING TIPS, opened it, and fished around inside until she found the folder she was looking for. On each page was a woman's face with a color wheel next to it. Mary Rose flipped through the folder until she found a beautiful red-headed, blue-eyed face with a color wheel that had different shades of green and blue in it.

"She doesn't look like you," said Veronica.

"Well, she's a grownup," Mary Rose said eagerly. "But I've got a lot of red in my hair, and my eyes are blue."

Veronica inspected Mary Rose's face. Her eyes certainly were blue, although the lady in the folder had deep blue eyes while Mary Rose's were pale. As for her hair, it was kind of blond and kind of brown, and the only red that Veronica could see was around Mary Rose's eyes from all the crying she'd been doing.

"Your hair's not red," she said.

"It is so," Mary Rose said passionately. "In the sun you can really see it, and it keeps growing redder all the time." She looked down at the color wheel, and said decisively, "Blue and green are my colors but I like blue better."

"I've got to do my homework," Veronica said, standing up.

Mary Rose said, "I think what I'd really like is a bed that had a blue satin spread over a white organdy skirt, and maybe a dressing table with a matching organdy skirt with blue satin bows."

Veronica picked up her books and walked to the door.

"An easy chair, painted a lighter blue, with matching upholstery," Mary Rose was murmuring happily as Veronica left the room. She walked through the living room, past Stanley still at the window, and back into the kitchen.

Mama was through soaking her feet, and was sitting at the table reading the newspaper. Veronica sat down across from her, opened her French book, and began studying.

"What are you doing, Veronica?" Mama said, startled.

"Studying."

"Studying?"

"Uh huh."

"That's nice," Mama said approvingly.

"*Avez-vous des livres?*" Veronica intoned softly. "*Oui, monsieur, j'ai plus de livres que vous. Avez-vous*

*des crayons? Non, monsieur, je n'ai pas de crayons
mais j'ai beaucoup de plumes. Avez-vous des chats?
Oui, monsieur, j'ai quelques—*"

"What's that you're saying?" Mama asked.

"Oh, I'm just reading the lesson in the book."

"Say it out loud," Mama urged.

Veronica said, "*Avez-vous des chats? Oui, monsieur, j'ai quelques chats.*"

"What does it mean?"

"It means," Veronica explained, "'Do you have any
cats? Yes, sir, I have a few cats.'"

"My!" Mama was impressed. "Say something else."

Veronica read, "*Avez-vous de l'argent? Oui, monsieur, mais j'ai peu d'argent.*"

"And what does that mean?"

"It means, 'Do you have any money? Yes, sir, but
I have a little bit of money.'"

Mama laughed. "It's the same in every language,"
she said, "but it's wonderful the way you say it,
Veronica. You sound like you really are French."

"It's easy," Veronica said carelessly.

Mama said proudly, "I always knew you had a
good head on your shoulders, Veronica. If you'd just
settle down and pay attention in school, you could
be as good as anybody else."

Veronica began intoning the next phrase. "*Avez-
vous du sucre?*"

"No reason why you shouldn't finish high school
—I only wish I had. I want the three of you to

finish school. And who knows, if we can afford it, maybe you could even go to college."

"*Oui, monsieur,*" Veronica murmured, "*j'ai trop de sucre.*"

Mama looked at the clock. "Seven o'clock," she said. "Ralph should be home soon. He's talking to Mr. Reyes, the owner of that radio store next to ours. It's going to be empty next month, and I told Ralph maybe we could rent it and expand the store. Business is pretty good now, and we could handle even more if we had more room."

"*Avez-vous des fleurs?*"

"We could hire another man," Mama said thoughtfully, "fix up the store, put in some new fixtures, paint it a nice color, and who knows, we just might make a go of it." She smiled at Veronica. "If we had some money, maybe we could even get a piano, and let you and Mary Rose take music lessons. It's a good thing for a girl to play the piano."

"*Oui, monsieur, j'ai plusieurs fleurs.*"

"Just listen to the way you say that," Mama said proudly. "Say that over again, that bit about do you have any money."

"*Avez-vous de l'argent?*" Veronica repeated. "*Oui, monsieur, mais j'ai peu d'argent.*"

Mama laughed again. She put her elbows on top of her newspaper and rested her face in her hands. "We just might make a go of it," she said dreamily, and her blue eyes had a happy, faraway look. She looked just like Mary Rose over her color charts.

Veronica read the next phrase. "*Avez-vous d'idées? Oui, monsieur, j'ai beaucoup des idées.*" I sure have, Veronica thought, smiling contentedly, plenty of ideas. Her eyes rested on her French book, but her ideas, in English, carried her off to an empty place filled only with the presence of Peter Wedemeyer. All alone there, they stood, the two of them, and as Veronica raised her clenched fist over Peter Wedemeyer's face, Mama's voice floated above them, ". . . and we'll buy a new bed for Stanley."

9

"Les anges dans nos campagnes
Ont entonné l'hymne des cieux"

sang Veronica with enthusiasm. In front of her, Reba
Fleming's red curls jiggled enticingly on her back,
and Veronica resisted a powerful impulse to yank.
Earlier, during that sappy country dance, while she
and Paul Lucas were whirling around onstage, she
had fought down a similarly powerful impulse to
pick him up and fling him off the stage.

This was the second Friday of rehearsals for the
French program that Veronica had attended. During
the first, she had done all the necessary research, and
today she was prepared to act. First there had been

the dances, then the carols. Next would come the play, *The Elves and the Shoemaker,* or to say it in French, *Les Elfes et le Cordonnier,* in which Peter played the shoemaker, and in which she had no role, thank goodness. The last item on the program was "Bring a Torch, Jeanette Isabella," or, *"Un Flambeau, Jeanette Isabella."* The whole group was supposed to take part in that—there were twenty-three children who had offered themselves for the program—and they were supposed to move slowly across the darkened stage in single file, singing. On the day of the performance, they would carry lighted flashlights swathed in orange tissue paper to look like torches. Honestly, how nutty could you get!

But anyway, last week she had done the research, and today was the day. Veronica grinned contentedly and raised the volume of her singing. What a stir it had created when she turned up for the rehearsals last Friday! Madame Nusinoff tried to act like it was perfectly natural, but boy, was she ever surprised! Veronica could see that. She could also see how the kids were trying to figure it out. Lorraine Jacobs kept poking Frances Scanlon with her elbow, and motioning with her head in Veronica's direction. She'd heard whispers and giggles, and figured they all had to do with her. When the rehearsals were over, Peter Wedemeyer had gone flying out of the auditorium ahead of everybody else, but she, instead of taking after him, had calmly remained in her seat until most of the kids had left. Nobody could tell

him that she was chasing him that day. No sir, she'd
been doing research that day, and today was the
day.

> *"Et l'écho de nos montagnes*
> *Redit ce chant mélodieux"*

Veronica sang, and looked at the clock on the
back wall of the auditorium. Four o'clock. Great!
Right on time. The play would take about half an
hour, and "Jeanette Isabella" about fifteen minutes.
So give or take a few minutes here and there, by four
forty-five the group would be out of the building and
on its way home.

"No, no, no!" Madame Nusinoff said suddenly. She
stopped playing the piano and stood up. "You're all
mumbling. The only one I can hear clearly is Veronica." She smiled approvingly at Veronica, and Veronica grinned back. Buddy, buddy, that's what she
and Madame Nusinoff were. And after today, she
wouldn't be coming back. But she knew the songs
all right. She'd memorized all of them. She wasn't
going to have Madame Nusinoff suspicious and throw
her out before she was ready to go.

Madame Nusinoff made them sing *"Les Anges dans
Nos Campagnes"* over again, and then that was that
for the carols.

"All right now," Madame Nusinoff said, "will the
children in the play get onstage, and the rest of you
come and sit down until the last number."

Veronica raised her right hand high. She wanted everybody to see and hear her. Her left hand she held behind her with two fingers crossed.

"What is it, Veronica?" Madame Nusinoff said.

"I have to go to the dentist," Veronica said in a loud voice. "My mother's waiting for me."

"Well," Madame Nusinoff said, "you'll miss the rehearsal for '*Un Flambeau, Jeanette Isabella.*'"

"I studied the song," Veronica said, "so I know it."

"All right then," said Madame Nusinoff. "Just make sure you don't miss the rehearsal next Friday because it will be the last one before the performance."

"Yes, ma'am, I will," Veronica said, and uncrossed her fingers. She walked off the stage, picked up her coat and books, and without a look behind her hurried out of the auditorium. She tried to act as if she was in a big rush so that Peter would really figure she had to go to the dentist.

Down the stairs she raced, out into the yard, and through the gate. She knew just where she was going. Her plan was foolproof, and the climax was just forty-five minutes off—give or take a few minutes. She crossed the small street at 169th, and sat down on one of the benches in McKinley Square. The square was not, properly speaking, a square at all. It was more of a triangle, and from the crest of the triangle one had a complete view of the children coming from school. More important, the square and its surrounding territory were off school limits, so whatever she did to Peter Wedemeyer there could not be held against her by the school authorities.

Peter would have to pass this way. The Franklin Avenue exit would be closed by this time. She'd checked that out too. Yes, she'd done her research last week, and it would not be long now.

> *"Un flambeau, Jeanette Isabella*
> *Un flambeau, courrons au berceau"*

Veronica began singing. It really was a catchy tune. She put her books down on the bench, and rubbed her hands together. Boy it was cold! But that was a good thing, too, because aside from one old man who was reading his newspaper farther down the bench, she was the square's only occupant. Even the policeman on duty after school to help the children cross the street had departed. Yes, sir, it was going to be one great day!

Up 169th Street came a horse pulling a wagon filled with apples, oranges, and grapefruits. The driver pulled on the reins, made a deep grunting noise, and the wagon stopped on one side of the square. Veronica watched the driver put down the reins and settle himself more comfortably on his seat on top of the wagon. He took a brown paper bag from behind him and began eating a sandwich. Veronica licked her lips. She was hungry, and she wondered what kind of a sandwich the man was eating. She put her hand in her pocket and pulled out two pennies. Maybe she'd buy an apple. There was plenty of time before Peter arrived.

"Hey, mister," she called up to him as she approached the wagon, "can I have an apple for two cents?"

The man, chewing away steadily, reached behind him and handed her down an apple. She put the two pennies in his hand, and bit into her apple. Then she took a look at the horse. It was a dirty white one, and it had blinders on either side of its head. There was a deep sore over one of its legs. Veronica moved a little closer to the horse and looked at the sore. It wasn't bleeding, but it was angry-looking, and as she inspected it the horse suddenly began shivering.

"Hey, mister," Veronica yelled, "your horse hurt himself."

The man just kept on chewing his sandwich.

Veronica moved around closer to the horse's head. The horse looked straight ahead. She was just about to take another bite of her apple when the horse turned its head, regarded her, and then the apple, and whinnied.

I bet he's hungry, Veronica thought suddenly. She held out her apple, and the horse laid his mouth on it but did not bite it.

"Go ahead, eat it, go ahead," Veronica urged.

The horse lifted its head again and looked straight ahead.

"Hey, mister," Veronica shouted, "what's his name?"

"Whose name?" said the man.

"The horse's."

"How should I know?"

Veronica was shocked. "Didn't you give him a name?"

The man finished his sandwich, and then began taking money out of his pockets, counting it, and putting it into a little sack.

"Well?" said Veronica.

"Look, kid, go away," said the man. "I'm busy."

"But why didn't you give him a name?" Veronica insisted. "Everybody's got a name."

"He's not my horse," the man said with one of those cranky smiles grownups have when they're getting irritated. "I rent him, and I didn't ask what his name was."

"Nice horse, good horse," Veronica murmured to the horse. "I bet your name's Silver. Silver!" she called, "here, Silver, have some apple. It'll make you feel better." She held out the apple again, and again the horse laid its mouth on it but did not eat.

"Hey, mister," Veronica yelled, "doesn't he like apples?"

A grunt from above and nothing else.

"I think he's sick," Veronica continued. "You should do something about it."

The man put his money away, picked up the reins, and clicked to the horse.

"You ought to tell somebody to fix that sore on his leg," Veronica yelled as the wagon began moving.

"Sure, sure," the man said. "I'll tell his mother."

Veronica quickly took a few more bites of her apple, and then threw the core after the departing wagon. It hit one of the wheels, but the driver didn't seem to notice.

Still chewing, Veronica walked back to her post and settled herself comfortably on the bench. A couple of times she had to stand up to stamp her feet because it was so cold. After a while, the man farther down the bench got up, folded his newspaper, and walked off.

First she saw Frances Scanlon and Lorraine Jacobs walking along. Then another girl, and behind her, a group of boys. Peter was one of them. Veronica could see his brown jacket very clearly. She waited until he came up to the crossing. Paul Lucas and Bill Stover were with him, and they were all talking and laughing, and not one of them saw her.

She stood up, and as Peter was halfway across the street, he saw her. So did Paul and Bill. Paul began moving backward, and she saw Peter take his arm and say something to him. Quickly she moved to the corner. If he ran, she'd get him anyway. But Peter did not run. He and the other two boys crossed the street and came right up to her.

"I've been waiting for you, Peter," Veronica said, leering, and she reached out to grab his jacket.

"O.K., boys, let's go!" Peter shouted, and suddenly

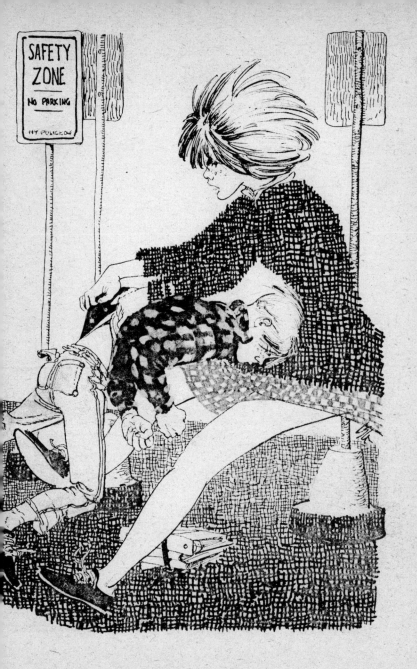

all three of them were on her, punching and butting and kicking.

Veronica managed to free herself, and she shouted at them, outraged, "That's not fair, three against one."

"So is it fair for you to beat up kids smaller than yourself?" said Peter.

"Paul Lucas"—Veronica shouted at him because his eyes were blinking nervously, and she knew what a coward he was—"I'll get you for this."

"No you won't," said Peter, beginning to move in on her. "Because from now on, any kid you beat up, the rest of us will get you."

And then they were all at her again. She popped Paul Lucas one right in the mouth, and heard him cry out. Then Peter was punching her from the front and Bill Stover from the back, and after a while, Paul Lucas returned, jabbing at her from all sides.

"You're all cowards," she shouted, but they were pummeling her and pushing her so hard that down she went with the three boys on top of her. Somebody was holding her hands, and somebody was sitting on her chest, and somebody was smacking her. And worst of all was the terrible knowledge that Peter had outfoxed her again.

Suddenly it was over, and a voice was shouting, "Stop it! Stop it!"

Her nose was bleeding. Her mouth was bleeding. One eye had funny lights in it, and the rest of her face felt raw and fiery. A man was picking her up, brushing her off, and talking all the time. "Ashamed of yourselves. I saw it all from across the street. The three of you against one girl—never saw such a thing in my life. Are you all right, honey?"

The man, a big, husky one, had Bill Stover by the collar, and after he had helped Veronica up, he grabbed Peter Wedemeyer. "I ought to report you to the police—a bunch of hoodlums."

"Mister, please listen, mister," Peter said. "You just don't understand."

"What's to understand?" shouted the man. "Three boys against one girl. Even for one boy to hit one girl—that's a disgrace. Didn't your parents ever tell you not to hit girls?"

"But, mister," Peter cried, "she hits us. She beats us up. She's bigger and stronger than anybody else in the class, and none of us have a chance against her. She's the biggest bully in the world. Ask anybody—"

And then all three boys began talking at once. It wasn't very clear what they were saying, but the passion in their voices seemed to confuse the man, and he turned to look at Veronica.

She did something then she had never done before in her whole life. She didn't know why she did it. She hadn't planned on doing it. It just seemed to happen without her even thinking. She sniffed, and a little sob broke from her throat.

And that seemed to decide it. Wondering, Veronica stood by and watched as the man shook each boy, banged their heads together, threatened to call the police if it happened again, and finally chased them away.

"I just don't know what this world is coming to," he said savagely as he made her sit down on the bench and lean back to stop her nose from bleeding. Carefully he touched the bruised spots on her cheeks and lips with his handkerchief. "A defenseless girl. You better tell your mother to come to school and tell the principal."

The man offered to accompany Veronica home just in case "those bullies" made a surprise attack on the way. But Veronica said she was sure they would not, thanked the man for his protection, and promised to tell her mother.

She would certainly have to tell Mama something she thought as she began walking home. The bruises all over her face would require some kind of explanation, and she was even tempted to follow her protector's advice and ask Mama to come to school to complain. That would be a new experience all around.

Veronica shook her head, and tried to collect her thoughts. She felt dazed and confused. Her face was a mess and her right shoulder ached fiercely. But something had happened today that had never happened before. Somebody had taken her part in a fight. Somebody had rescued her. Somebody had tended to her bruises and sent her on her way with kind words instead of insults. Why?

Wasn't she the same person she had always been?

What had made this time different from all other times? And why was she feeling so happy? Peter had beaten her or had he? He had outfoxed her, and he and his friends had beaten her up. That was certainly so. She had been defeated and yet—she was the winner. She knew she was the winner, and suddenly she knew why.

Peter's strategy had really been brilliant. She had to hand it to him. He had organized a vigilante committee against her, and he had been right in figuring she would be defenseless against it. But he had overlooked one important fact—and it was something she had never until today appreciated. The weapon she had been searching for was one she had possessed all along, and one which she had never used before. Peter had gone down to defeat—not because she was stronger than he, or smarter, but because of something more powerful than that. She was a girl. And it was a mighty thing being a girl.

10

Mama and Mary Rose were going at it hot and heavy when she arrived home. Mary Rose was crying and Mama was shouting, and nobody noticed the condition of her face except for Stanley.

"Wow!" he cried when she walked through the door. "What happened to you, Veronica?"

Mama was screaming, "You have no right opening my letters. I don't care who it's from. If you couldn't wait until I got home, you should have brought it over to the store. I'm not going to stand for this. I'm—"

"I wish I was dead!" Mary Rose sobbed.

Veronica walked around both of them, and into the bathroom. What a day! She put her books down

on the floor and looked at her face in the mirror of
the medicine cabinet. "Wow!" was right. She ran
the water in the sink and washed off all the blood
from her face. While she was drying it, the voices
outside grew louder. Then there was a thump, and
a loud howl from Mary Rose. Mama must have
whacked her one. Veronica hung up her towel and
returned to the living room. What was it all about
this time?

Mama had Mary Rose by the shoulder, and was
shaking her, and saying, "Never again! If you ever
do it again, I'll—"

Mary Rose was sobbing and struggling, and then
suddenly Mama stopped shouting. All of a sudden,
she just lifted Mary Rose up, carried her over to
the chair, and sat down with her in her lap. She
began rocking her back and forth in her arms,
and—figure that out—she began kissing her over and
over again. She didn't say anything—just kept kissing
Mary Rose, and Mary Rose put her arms around
Mama's neck, and instead of sobbing, began a low
whining.

"What's going on here?" Veronica demanded.

But Mama and Mary Rose were still all wrapped
up in each other, and it was Stanley who answered
her.

"He's not coming, and Mary Rose opened Mama's
letter, and Mama was mad, and—"

"Who's not coming?" said Veronica, but she knew
very well who it was.

"Your Papa," Stanley said. "He sent money."

Mama began talking to Mary Rose then. "Don't feel bad, sweetie," she said. "We're really going to have a good time during Christmas vacation. Maybe I'll even take you all down to Radio City, and we'll have lunch in the Automat."

Mary Rose didn't say anything. Just kept her face buried in Mama's shoulder.

Mama sighed. "Look, sweetie"—imagine Mama calling Mary Rose sweetie!—"he really wanted to come. He cares for you. He really does, but he just doesn't have the money."

Mary Rose said in a muffled voice, her face still hidden on Mama's shoulder, "I thought he had a lot of money. I thought he was rich."

"Now where did you ever get that idea?" Mama said, smoothing Mary Rose's hair.

Mary Rose didn't answer the question. Veronica looked at her sister's back with sympathy but with a feeling of righteousness too. Of course she couldn't answer Mama's question. What was she going to say—that she'd been listening behind closed doors, that she'd been eavesdropping, hearing everything wrong.

"No," Mama said. "He tried to open a restaurant in Las Vegas, and it didn't work out. So now he's working for somebody else, and he just doesn't have the money to come. But he wanted to," she added quickly. "You can see how disappointed he sounds—and look—he sent five dollars for you and five dollars for Veronica."

Veronica had a pretty good idea what was going to happen to the five dollars for Mary Rose and the five dollars for her. Mama would go and buy them underwear and pajamas—things like that. Any time their Papa sent them money Mama always frittered it away on useful things.

"And you know what?" Mama said cheerfully. "You can buy anything you like with the money."

"Really?" said Veronica. And she knew exactly what she was going to do with it. She was going to take it over to the bicycle store on Third Avenue where they sold second-hand bikes. For five dollars or maybe six—and she could always raise another dollar—she'd have her own bike. What a day this was turning out to be. "Really?" she said again, stretching her sore mouth into a painful grin.

Mary Rose raised her head from Mama's shoulder. "Anything I like?" she said.

"Uh huh." Mama smiled.

"Well," Mary Rose said, breathing fast. "There's a gorgeous blue bedspread in Alexander's. I think it's satin with white flowers embroidered all over it. It's the most gorgeous thing I ever saw in my whole life."

"Satin?" Mama said, dismayed.

"And there's curtains to match—such stunning curtains—with scallops on the bottom and, oh, Mama, it's the most . . . most . . . just out of this world."

"How much?"

"Five dollars for the bedspread and five for the drapes."

She looked at Veronica.

"I'm buying a bike," Veronica announced.

Mary Rose's face fell.

Mama said, "Well, you can buy the bedspread with your five dollars, and—now I'm not promising anything—but—well, I haven't bought your Christmas present yet—and if you think you'd rather have the drapes than anything else, maybe—and I'm not promising . . ."

Mary Rose's eyes began shining.

"I'm buying a bike," Veronica repeated.

Mama looked at her, and then took another look. "What happened to you?" she shouted.

And it was a good thing that Mary Rose was around, because before Veronica had a chance to really think up a good story, Mary Rose started gabbing again about how she'd like to fix up the room. Then she ran off and brought back her box of decorating tips and began showing Mama all the junk she had collected there. Soon the two of them were talking away and Mama had forgotten all about Veronica.

She walked off to the bedroom, and Stanley followed her.

"Veronica," he said, his face glowing, "I made something for Papa in school today. I'm going to give it to him for Christmas."

"That's nice," Veronica said, hanging up her coat in the closet.

Stanley waited for a moment, and then he said, "Veronica!"

"What?"

"You want to know what it is?"

"O.K.," Veronica said, hunting around on the dresser for a bobby pin. Her hair was flopping around over her eyes.

"You won't tell anybody?"

Veronica found a pin, and shoved it through her hair on one side of her head, and began hunting for another pin.

"You promise, Veronica?"

"O.K., O.K.," Veronica said impatiently. "What is it?"

Stanley looked around him, shut the door, and tiptoed over to her. He put up his face, and she bent down and put her ear up close to his mouth.

"It's a Santa Claus on a string," Stanley whispered.

"Oh!" said Veronica, beginning to straighten up, but Stanley held her down, and continued whispering. "When you jiggle the string, the Santa Claus dances up and down."

Stanley's breath was warm in her ear, and he smelled different from the way older people smelled—a special kind of young smell like—like fresh coconut.

So she said enthusiastically, "Oh, that's great! He'll love that," and rubbed his nose with the palm of her hand, and then pinched his little backside.

Stanley glowed. "What are you getting everybody for Christmas, Veronica?" he asked.

"I don't know. I haven't thought about it yet."

"Look," said Stanley, fishing down in his pocket, "look what I got." He drew out some change and showed it to her. "Sixteen cents. Take me over to Woolworth's, Veronica."

"I will tomorrow," Veronica said, smiling at him. "Where'd you get all that money?"

"I've been saving it," Stanley said, "so now I can buy presents for Mama and Mary Rose and you. Let's go now, Veronica."

"But it's nearly six o'clock," Veronica said weakly.

"They're open late today," Stanley pleaded. "Please, Veronica. If you take me, Mama'll let me go."

"Well, O.K.," Veronica said. She and Stanley walked back into the living room. Mary Rose was showing Mama a chart of paint colors, and saying, "We could paint all the furniture white, and buy a white lampshade for the lamp, and . . ."

Mama was shaking her head, and Veronica said, "Stanley and I are going out for a little while."

"What time is it?" Mama said.

"Nearly six."

"I'm going to make supper now." Mama began rising.

"The paint won't cost much," Mary Rose insisted.

"But not white," Mama said. "That would show

up a lot of dirt. Why don't you just leave it the
way it is, and one of these days maybe we'll be able
to buy some new furniture."

"We'll be back soon," said Veronica.

"You always say that," continued Mary Rose,
"but you never have the money. So let me paint it,
and it'll look like new, and you won't have to buy
new furniture."

"Please, Mama, can we go?" said Stanley.

"Uh," said Mama, looking at Mary Rose, then at
Stanley, and then at Veronica.

"We'll be back in half an hour," said Veronica.

"If you don't like white," Mary Rose compro-
mised, "how about blue?"

"All right," said Mama. "I mean all right, Veronica,
but don't stay out long, and pick up two quarts of
milk at the grocery store."

"Come on, Stanley," Veronica said.

"How about blue?" demanded Mary Rose.

Woolworths was a blazing glitter of Christmas
colors. There were wreaths, and paper bells, and
tinsel, and brilliant Christmas balls swinging above
and around them. Stanley took a deep, happy breath,
and proceeded down the aisles, followed by Veronica. At every counter he paused, and ran his hand
lovingly up and down everything within reach—boxes
of face powder, papers of needles, thimbles, powder puffs, back scratchers, pads of paper, erasers,
little lavender bags of sachet. There were so many
things to consider, but, finally, with Veronica's help,

he decided on a small candy dish for Mama. It cost five cents. Then the fingering and deliberation for Mary Rose's gift began. Veronica ambled along behind him, waiting while he considered a package of six pencils in assorted colors, a silver key ring, a Christmas glitter pin, a coloring book, a fancy blue garter, a large package of gummed address labels, a small package of balloons, and a spool of bright red string for Mary Rose's horse rein. Again with Veronica acting as consultant, he finally decided on an attractive horse-shaped pack of pen wipers.

"Do you really think that's what she wants?" Stanley asked.

"Oh, she'll love it," Veronica said heartily. "She really needs it."

Stanley paid the saleslady a nickel, then he looked mysteriously at Veronica and said, "You go away now. I'm going to look around myself."

Now he was going to buy her a gift, so Veronica said sweetly, "O.K., but don't take too long."

Stanley nodded, and scooted away. Veronica began wandering up and down the aisles, luxuriating in the sense of well-being that she always felt in Woolworths. On all sides of her were displayed shining new articles—all desirable and all lying there waiting for her. She lingered by the ribbon counter, running her finger over the roll of red velvet ribbon and inhaling the delicious smell of Woolworth's— part chocolate and part talcum powder.

A few aisles away she caught a glimpse of Stanley's head bent over something, and she felt a glow of pleasure. Stanley was buying a present for her. Of course it was only going to be a nickel present, but still and all it was always exciting when you knew somebody was buying you a present and you didn't know what it was going to be.

Lazily she moved over to the cosmetics counter, and thought that she'd have to do some Christmas shopping herself. It was always a snap getting something for Mama. Women were easier to buy presents for than men. There was a pretty bottle of blue bath salts decorated with a fancy red ribbon on display that caught her eye. Bath salts looked enticing and colorful in the bottle, but they were always a disappointment when you put them in the tub. Nothing much happened. Maybe she'd buy perfume for Mama this year. There now, for twenty-nine cents, she could get Mama that box of six small bottles of flower perfumes. Lilac, said one, Lilies of the Valley said another, Violets, Heliotrope—now what was Heliotrope? She didn't know what Heliotrope smelled like but it sounded lovely . . . Apple Blossom, Forget-me-not.

Dreamily, Veronica moved to the jewelry counter and stood admiring the collection of birthstone rings. Garnets for January, amethysts for February, aquamarines for March, diamonds for April—no one was left out. There was something here for everybody.

Veronica thought—what if I was locked in here all by myself? What if the place closed for a few weeks and nobody knew I was here—it would all belong to me—the yards of lace and ribbon, the snake plants, the candy. She'd have blankets to cover herself at night, games to play with all day, perfumes—Heliotrope and Forget-me-not—to put in one of those spray bottles and spray herself with, paintings to look at, counters and counters of strange unfamiliar wonders to discover, jewelry to wear. She reached out and picked up a gleaming ruby ring for July—her month, and slipped it on her finger. I'd be a queen in Woolworth's. No—better than a queen because there wouldn't be anyone around to bother me.

She held out her finger and looked into the depths of the gleaming ruby, and saw herself peering out of its depths. Not with a black eye and a swollen mouth, because that was all far away and had no place here. Maybe in that world outside there were big girls, bigger than anyone else, who beat up small boys. And maybe there were small boys, smaller than anyone else, who tried to beat up big girls. And maybe there were questions that had to be thought about. But not now. Because here in Woolworth's nobody fought, and nobody was hurt, and nobody struggled to understand. There was only a blazing ruby on her finger, and her own face looking up at her, silent and serene.

"Yes?" said a cheery voice. "Can I help you?"

Veronica turned, and blinked in the direction of the voice. A saleslady stood behind the counter waiting. "Do you want that?" she continued, gesturing toward the ring on Veronica's finger.

"Uh, no," Veronica said slowly. "I'll—uh—get it next time I come."

The saleslady silently and emphatically held out her hand. Veronica slipped off the ring, laid it in the woman's palm, and hurried off to find Stanley.

He was standing near the candy counter, looking at her.

"Are you finished, Stanley?" Veronica said. They'd been in Woolworth's much longer than the half hour she had promised Mama. The clock over the door said seven-fifteen.

Stanley was holding a bag in his hand, and his face had a tormented expression.

"Veronica," he said, looking as if he was going to burst into tears.

"What?" she said sharply, eyeing the bag in his hand. It was a bag of candy, she realized, feeling a flash of resentment. He'd gone and spent her nickel, her Christmas present money, on a bag of candy for himself.

"Veronica," Stanley repeated, beginning to hiccup, "you know that Santa—*hic*—Claus I made for Papa? Well—*hic*—do you think I could give it to two people for Christmas—*hic*?"

The world outside was already here, but a faint glow still surrounded her from out of the depths of the ruby. The nickel was spent, wasn't it? And after all just how much could you expect from a five-year-old anyway, especially one like Stanley? So she just shook her head at him, swallowed her disappointment, and said, "Sure you could, Stanley, sure—and stop hiccuping."

Stanley smiled, and picked a malted milk ball out of the bag, and popped it into his mouth. "Here, Veronica," he said, holding out the bag to her, "take a candy. Go on. Take two candies."

11

So if everything was so good, why was she feeling so bad? Veronica leaned against the school fence in her usual position and knew that everything was wrong. Here she'd been waiting for this moment all weekend, thought about it, arranged it in her mind, rearranged it, gloated over it—and it wasn't happening at all the way it was supposed to.

First of all, Peter wasn't even here. Depend on him! It would be just like him to go ahead and be sick and not show up at all. She had thought about his face over the past two days, and had looked at it in her mind from all sorts of angles—front, profile, three-quarter view, back and then front, front and then side, looking down, looking up. But every way she saw it, Peter's expression was the same—a combination of anger and humiliation.

She had come to school this Monday morning in fine spirits and with a new sense of her own powers. Veronica bounced her body backward into the wire gate, felt it respond, and wondered what she could do *now*. Paul Lucas and Bill Stover were around. She'd seen them as soon as she arrived, and they'd seen her. Which was probably why they were nowhere in sight at the present moment. Sissies! Who cared about them! But Peter—she couldn't wait to see Peter's face. Of course she knew exactly what her own face would look like. Peter would look at her. There would be fury and shame and revenge written on his face. But her face—too bad her left eye was still so black and blue, and her mouth all swollen—would remain silent and serene. She'd practiced that silent and serene look in the mirror over the weekend, and had really worked it into something splendid.

Her eyes explored the yard once more, probing carefully into some of the usually neglected corners. Peter was nowhere. So what was there to do? There wasn't anybody she was after. For ages now, Peter alone had occupied all her attention. Peter singing those silly jingles about her. Peter laughing at her, playing tricks on her, tormenting her while she prowled and plotted revenge.

What *was* there to do? Veronica slowly bounced several more times against the gate, then stood up, and began moving aimlessly toward the center of the yard. Linda Jensen and Frieda Harris were bouncing a ball, playing "A My Name Is," and Frieda was up to E. She was saying, "Edith Edison eats eggs every Easter evening but Eddie Edison eats eggplant," and turning her foot over the ball on every word that started with "E." "That's more than ten," she said, stopping and preparing to go on to "F." Then she noticed Veronica watching. She looked in a worried way at Linda. Linda said, her forehead wrinkling, "Uh . . . do you want to play, Veronica?"

"Naa," said Veronica.

So Frieda began bouncing the ball again, saying, "Frances Farmer fixes frankfurters Friday," but she was saying it too fast, and she missed, and the ball went bouncing away. While she was chasing it, Veronica moved off, and paused to watch a rope game in progress. There were about eight girls jumping, and two girls turning. Reba Fleming had landed on "Z," and so the group chanted as she jumped, "H—O—T spells HOT." The enders began turning very quickly, and Reba jumped faster and faster as the group counted ten, twenty, thirty, forty, fifty, sixty, seventy, eighty. Reba missed on eighty so she had to take one of the ends. She saw Veronica standing there, looked around at the other girls, and said nervously, "If you like, you can get on line."

"Naa," said Veronica.

The game started up again, and after a while Veronica wandered off, stopping to watch a bunch of other children playing "Follow the Leader." Rita Ferguson saw her first, looked meaningfully at Frances Scanlon, jerked her head in Veronica's direction, and said, "Hi . . . uh, Veronica, do you feel like playing with us?"

There was nothing to do, absolutely nothing. And Veronica, feeling unhappy and very lonely, was just about to say, "Naa," and move on, when she caught sight of Peter, leaning against the fence and looking right at her. This was the moment she'd been waiting for—the moment when she was supposed to look back at him, silent and serene. But she felt embarrassed, and instead, cried heartily, "Sure, I'll play. Sure." She added her books to the row already on the ground and took her place at the end of the line. Soon she was leaping, laughing, and generally trying to give the impression that she was having the time of her life. Every so often, she'd look up quickly at Peter, and each time he was exactly in the same place, leaning against the fence and staring at her.

When Hilda Rosenzweig became leader, and was rearranging all the books, lunch boxes, rulers, and jackets to form a new hurdle, and the rest of them stood around waiting, Rita Ferguson moved cautiously closer to Veronica to get a better view of her black eye.

Veronica's good eye noted Peter as he bounced against the wire gate, looked toward her, bounced again, looked again. . . . There was an agonizing desire inside her to share all this with somebody else, somebody who could enjoy with her all the details of Peter's humiliation, all the excitement and suspense of the present moment.

She looked hungrily at Rita, and Rita looked hungrily into her black eye. Should she tell her? Rita's eyes were traveling happily down Veronica's scratched nose, settling finally with satisfaction on her swollen lips. No! She wouldn't tell Rita anything. Rita would only enjoy the fact that she had been beaten.

Hilda Rosenzweig finished her arrangements—the hurdle now curved like an S—and shouted, "O.K., let's go!" As the line braced itself, Veronica saw Peter throw himself into one fierce bounce against the gate, stand up, and head in her direction. Veronica's fists clenched. Desperately she thought, No! I don't want to fight. But what should I do? Where should I go? She looked around, but nobody noticed. Nobody realized what was happening. The bell rang. Peter stopped in his tracks, looked at her, and then headed over to the boy's line.

All morning long Peter watched her, circled, approached, retreated, and instead of feeling easy and triumphant, Veronica was confused and filled with an unfamiliar sense of panic. What should she do? Madame Nusinoff asked her to remain after French class. It was only to tell her what the group had decided in the way of costumes, since she had missed the discussion last Friday afternoon. And as Madame Nusinoff talked about flare skirts for the dances, and artificial flowers on crepe-paper streamers for the girls' hair, Veronica looked longingly into the teacher's face, waiting for her to stop talking.

Madame Nusinoff stopped finally. She looked at Veronica's black eye, and her own eyes, like Rita's, moved across Veronica's bruised nose and down to her swollen lips. Madame Nusinoff did not look pleased, as Rita had. She looked troubled, and said gently, "What happened, Veronica?"

Veronica hesitated. Then she shook her head. "Nothing," she said, and hurried off to her next class. What's the use, she thought to herself. She'd never believe me anyway.

At lunch, Peter, Paul, and Bill sat together, looking over at her. During the afternoon recess, Veronica saw them again, whispering and staring at her. They would be waiting for her this afternoon, she knew now for sure. Perhaps this time there would be no one around to help. Perhaps there would. If so, would they wait for her again tomorrow? The next day? Would it go on and on until they were able to get her alone somewhere and beat her up without anybody stepping in and breaking it up. And wasn't this what she would do if she was after somebody? But she wasn't after anybody, and how

silly she had been to think that after Friday everything would be better. Things were worse—and
she was now the hunted instead of the hunter. And
even worse than that was this terribly lonely feeling
that had held on to her all through the day.

Veronica left by way of the Franklin Avenue
exit that afternoon, and went home the long way.

Peter was standing on her stoop, waiting for her.
She looked around for Paul and Bill, but they were
not in sight. As soon as he saw her, Peter jumped off
the stoop and came flying toward her. It was too
late to run. He was standing there in front of her.
He stuck his face right up close to hers, and
shouted, "Go ahead! Sock me!"

Veronica looked quickly behind her. Nobody in
sight yet. "Sure," she cried, "that's all I have to do.
And I know what'll happen next."

"What?" shouted Peter.

"Where are Paul and Bill?" said Veronica, looking
over his shoulder.

Peter's face turned a deep red. He backed away,
and said, "Nobody's here but me."

"Sure, sure," Veronica said, looking across the
street.

"I swear to God," Peter went on fervently. "All
weekend long, I kept thinking about it, and I don't
know why I did it. That man was right. It's bad
enough for a boy to hit a girl, but for three boys
to gang up on one girl, even a girl like you . . ."
Peter's voice cracked. His face was exactly what she

had hoped to see—filled with anger and humiliation. But instead of feeling triumphant, Veronica felt embarrassed, and even more lonely.

"What do you mean—a girl like me?" she cried. I never did anything to you. You were the one who started it."

Peter shook his head impatiently. "Well, everybody said you were such a bully—always picking on kids smaller than yourself."

"But everybody is smaller than me," Veronica said helplessly, "and what am I supposed to do if they make fun of me?"

"But you're so big," Peter said, looking up at her with a strange look on his face.

"I know I'm big," Veronica shouted. "That's the whole trouble. I just wish I was small like everybody else."

"But why?" Peter said, screwing up his face in surprise.

"So nobody would make fun of me."

"But why should you care?" said Peter. "If I was like you, I wouldn't care what anybody said. You're such a . . . such a . . . big girl."

"Stop saying that!" Veronica said between her teeth.

"You're the biggest girl I know," Peter said solemnly.

"Do you want me to sock you?" Veronica cried desperately, clenching her fists.

"Yes, that's right," Peter nodded. "I forgot. I

want you to sock me. And I swear to God, I'll never raise my hand to you again no matter what happens. Even though you're so big, you're still a girl, so go ahead! Sock me!" Peter moved in closer, and stuck his face out again.

So it was all going to be over then—finished. Peter would never tease her or hound her, and probably not even notice her any more. And why? Because she was a girl. Well, she'd show him. Even if she was a girl, she could still punch him so hard he'd never forget it. She raised her fist and—nothing happened.

"I'm not going to sock you," Veronica yelled, feeling as if she was going to cry. "Leave me alone! Go away!"

But Peter kept moving in closer, saying in a soft, wheedling voice, "Go ahead, Veronica, just sock me, a good hard one. I've got it coming, and I won't hit you back."

"No, no, no!" Veronica cried, retreating. Nothing was right today. Everything was upside down.

Peter said, "Look, I'll put one hand behind my back so you don't have to be afraid. Go ahead. Hit me!"

Veronica reached the edge of the sidewalk, and put one foot off the curb. Peter put his hand behind his back, closed his eyes, and stood, chin out, waiting. The top of his head came up to her mouth, and the rest of him looked so small and slight that it seemed to her that all she'd have to do was breathe hard on him, and he'd fall down.

"Don't be afraid," he repeated. "My hand's behind my back."

"Your hand's behind your back," Veronica repeated, feeling something beginning to tingle inside her, "behind your back."

Peter opened his eyes.

"Why if I wanted to . . ." Veronica began, but then she was laughing so hard she couldn't talk. Behind his back! Little Peter Wedemeyer was going to *let* her hit him! Little Peter Wedemeyer had put his hand behind his back so she shouldn't be afraid of *him*. It was too much. Veronica sank to the ground, laughing and laughing and laughing.

"What's so funny?" shouted Peter.

"Oh . . . behind your back . . ." gasped Veronica.

"Look—are you going to hit me?" demanded Peter.

"Oh . . . oh . . . oh . . ." laughed Veronica, doubled up.

"Drop dead!" Peter yelled, and began walking away.

Veronica continued laughing until her breath was gone. Then she slowly rose to her feet, looked back down the street, and saw Peter standing there, watching her. She began to laugh again, and had to lean against a lamppost to keep herself from falling.

Suddenly it started again. She stopped laughing and listened. Was he crazy? She clenched her fists and turned sharply. Peter was jumping up and down, shouting,

> *"You're in a trance,*
> *Veronica Ganz."*

Veronica started toward him, and watched as he scrambled for the corner. No! No! That's not what she wanted to do—not any more. So she stopped, and watched him scurry across the street. He turned on the other side, and shouted again,

> *"You're in a trance,*
> *Veronica Ganz."*

And then Veronica knew that everything was going to be all right. That it wasn't going to be all over. That Peter would go on teasing her for a long time to come. And that it was good. Because he wouldn't tease her if he didn't want to—not any more. Just listen to him yodeling across the street there. Maybe she was a girl, and maybe he was a boy. So what! Now she could admit to herself that of all the kids she'd ever met, Peter was the one she liked and admired the most, Peter, screeching over there at her from across the street—the little nut—screeching at HER. What a wonderful feeling it was to like somebody and know that he liked you too, that maybe he had liked you all along, even though you were a girl, even though you were such a big girl. And how could you show a person how you felt? How? Veronica thought hard for a moment, shook her head, thought again, and then leaned off the curb, cupped her hands around her mouth, and shouted,

> *"What a crier*
> *Is Peter Wedemeyer!"*

And as the small figure across the street clutched his head in mock despair and staggered backward, Veronica, excited and happy at what was just beginning, giggled like a girl.

```
  1979
-   32
────────
  1947


  1979
-   35
────────
  1944
```